Anna on the Farm

Anna on the Farm

by Mary Downing Hahn

illustrated by Diane de Groat

Clarion Books ◆ New York

Clarion Books
a Houghton Mifflin Company imprint
215 Park Avenue South, New York, NY 10003
Text copyright © 2001 by Mary Downing Hahn
Illustrations copyright © 2001 by Diane de Groat

The text was set in 14-point Garamond.
The illustrations were executed in pencil.

www.houghtonmifflinbooks.com

Printed in U.S.A.

Library of Congress Cataloging-in-Publication Data
Hahn, Mary Downing.
Anna on the farm / by Mary Downing Hahn.
p. cm.
Summary: Nine-year-old Anna is happy to spend a week at her aunt and
uncle's Beltsville, Maryland, farm until she meets Theodore, who calls her a
"city slicker" and spurs her to prove that she's just as clever and brave as he is.
ISBN 0-618-03605-9
[1. Farm life—Maryland—Fiction. 2. Friendship—Fiction.
3. Orphans—Fiction. 4. Maryland—Fiction.] I. Title.
PZ7.H1256 Ap 2001
[Fic]—dc21   00-043194

QUM   10   9   8   7   6   5   4   3   2   1

For Mom, *of course,*
and in memory of
Ira Plumley Sherwood,
20 January 1872 – 7 April 1920
and
Elisabeth Mary Sherwood,
26 October 1871 – 25 April 1947

Contents

1   Where Are You Going This Summer? 1

2   Bears, Wolves, and Snakes 12

3   "Good-bye, Baltimore!" 20

4   The First Night Away 34

5   Chores 42

6   Getting Even 51

7   Mud Monsters 62

8   Cousin Herman 70

9   Princess Nell 80

10   Trouble in the Barn 95

11   Market Day 114

12   The Church Supper 125

13   Home Again, Home Again 140

Where Are You Going This Summer?

Oꜱᴇ ꜱᴜᴍᴍᴇʀ ᴅᴀʏ, Aɴɴᴀ, Bᴇᴀᴛʀɪᴄᴇ, ᴀɴᴅ Rᴏꜱᴀ ᴀʀᴇ sitting on Anna's front steps, fanning themselves with old newspapers. The narrow brick houses crowd together, trapping the heat. No breeze blows. Even the pigeons waddle slowly, making sad cooing sounds.

Anna thinks Baltimore is the hottest city in the world. Just this morning Father said the sidewalk was hot enough to cook his breakfast. Anna wanted Mother to try frying eggs outside to keep the house cooler, but Mother told her that was a silly idea.

Beatrice and Rosa are playing cat's cradle with a

piece of string. As usual, Rosa is bossing Beatrice, telling her to hold her fingers still. Whenever the three girls are together, Rosa thinks of something only she and Beatrice can do. At least that's how it seems to Anna.

Anna sighs loudly, hoping to get the other girls' attention, but they are more interested in their stupid piece of string than they are in Anna. She looks across the street, hoping to see her friend Charlie. His little sisters and brothers are chasing each other up and down the sidewalk, but Charlie isn't there. Most likely he's playing ball with the neighborhood boys. Anna wishes she were playing ball, too. Anything would be more fun than sitting here watching Rosa and Beatrice.

Up the street Anna hears the melon man singsonging, "I got watermelons, watermelons, nice cold watermelons. Watermelons, watermelons."

Soon he comes nearer, leading a brown-and-white pony. The pony pulls a small yellow wagon piled high with watermelons. The pony's head droops, his hooves clip-clop slowly over the paving stones. He's hot, too.

The melon man passes Anna's house every day. Mother buys one watermelon a week, no more. The man tips his cap to the girls, but he does not stop. Mother bought her watermelon yesterday.

Anna wishes the wagon would hit a bump and a watermelon would fall off and roll right to her feet. She can almost taste it—cold and wet and sweet and pink, with hard black seeds to spit when Mother isn't looking.

The wagon rolls on down the hill toward North Avenue. No watermelons fall off. Anna sighs again. "It's so hot," she says loudly.

Rosa pushes her blond curls back from her round pink face. "Guess what? I'm going to the ocean next week. It will be much cooler there."

"I'm going to the mountains," Beatrice says quickly. "It will be even cooler there."

Rosa gives Beatrice's skinny arm a little pinch, just hard enough to hurt. "We're going to stay in the Henlopen Hotel," she brags. "It's the most expensive hotel in Rehoboth Beach. In the daytime, we'll wade in the surf and build sand castles. At dinner, we'll dress up in our best clothes. In the evening, we'll walk on the boardwalk and eat candy apples and frozen custard and saltwater taffy."

Anna's mouth waters. She's never eaten saltwater

taffy at the ocean. In fact, she's never even been to the ocean. She imagines it's like the Chesapeake Bay, only bigger. She hopes the water is full of jellyfish so Rosa will get stung while she's splashing in the water. It would serve the stuck-up thing right.

"We're going to Penmar on the train," Beatrice says quietly. "The air is very fresh in the mountains. Dr. Thompson says it will be good for my cough."

Both girls look at Anna. Everybody goes on vacation in August. They're waiting for her to tell them where her family is going. Instead, Anna bends her head and picks at a scab on her knee. The truth is she's not going anywhere. Father says they can't afford a vacation, but Anna doesn't want to admit this to Rosa and Beatrice.

"Well?" Rosa pokes her plump finger in Anna's ribs. "Where are *you* going?"

"We haven't decided yet," Anna says. "Mother likes the mountains and Father likes the ocean." This isn't exactly a lie. What she's said about Mother's and Father's likes and dislikes is true.

"Maybe you'll spend a week in the mountains *and* a week at the ocean," Beatrice says. "Wouldn't that be fun?"

Rosa gets to her feet. "Anna isn't going anywhere," she says. "Her mother and father probably can't afford a vacation."

Anna jumps up. "That's not true, Rosa!"

But Rosa is already walking down the hill toward her house. "Come on, Beatrice," she says. "Mother has promised to make nice cold lemonade and sugar cookies."

Beatrice hesitates, but Anna is too mad to care whether Beatrice goes or stays. Turning her back on both girls, she runs into her house and slams the door behind her.

Mother and Aunt May look up when Anna stamps crossly into the kitchen. They are having their afternoon coffee. Anna cannot imagine drinking something hot on a summer day, but Mother claims it makes you cooler.

"Your face is red," Aunt May says. "Are you coming down with something?"

Mother looks worried. "Come here, Anna, and let me feel your forehead," she says. "Just yesterday I saw a scarlet fever quarantine sign on a house on Bentalou Street."

"I'm not *sick* sick," Anna says, pulling away from Mother's hand. "Just sick of stupid stuck-up Rosa."

"My, my," Aunt May says, laughing. "So many *s*'s, *meine hübsche Kartoffel.* You sound like a hissing snake."

"It's not funny." Anna sticks out her lip. She isn't in the mood for Aunt May's little jokes or her funny German words. If her aunt wants to call Anna a smart potato, why can't she say it in English?

Before Mother can tell her to hush, Anna says, "Rosa's going to stay in a big fancy hotel in Rehoboth Beach, and Beatrice is taking a train to the mountains. But we're not going anywhere! It's not fair!" Anna knows she's speaking too loudly, but she can't help herself. She's so mad she even stamps her foot.

"Hush, Anna," Mother says. "I will not tolerate such rude talk. You know perfectly well we can't afford a vacation. I don't know where the Schumanns find the money for such foolishness. Vacations are for rich people."

Aunt May takes a sip of coffee. "Poor Anna," she says. "I know how you feel. I'd love to spend a week at the ocean myself."

Mother sighs. "I prefer the mountains. The sun is too hot at the ocean. It burns my skin."

"I don't care where I go," Anna says. "I just want to go somewhere!"

"Go? Where are you going, Anna?"

Anna turns and sees Father coming through the front door, home from his job at the newspaper.

"I want to go on a vacation like Rosa and Beatrice," Anna tells him. "To the ocean, to the mountains—I don't care which."

"How about Uncle George's farm for a week?" Father asks. "Would that do?"

Anna stares at Father, too surprised to speak. Mother and Aunt May also stare at Father, just as surprised as Anna.

"I talked to my sister today," Father tells Mother, smiling at Anna. "Aggie thought Anna might like to get away from the city for a while."

Anna hugs Father. "Yes, yes, yes!" she shouts, jumping up and down with excitement. She can hardly wait to see Aunt Aggie and Uncle George. "I'd love to go to the farm!"

Mother looks worried. "But Anna is a city girl," she says. "What will she do on a farm for a whole week? Suppose she falls and hurts herself? Suppose a cow tramples her? She might step on a rusty nail and get lockjaw, she might ruin her looks with freckles, she—"

Father pats Mother's shoulder. "Don't fret, Lizzie. Neither Aggie nor George will let Anna come to harm."

Aunt May agrees. "The farm will be good for Anna. Think of the fresh air, Lizzie—fresh milk, fresh eggs, and fresh vegetables, too. All that freshness will put roses in Anna's cheeks and flesh on her skinny little bones."

"It's not as if Anna is going to the end of the earth," Father puts in. "George's farm is only twenty miles away. We've been there together many times. Now Anna will go without us, but she's nine years old—just the right age for an adventure."

Mother sighs. With both Father and Aunt May in favor of the farm, she's losing the argument. "I suppose you're right," she says slowly. "Anna is pale and much too thin. Perhaps the farm is just what she needs."

Although Anna doesn't like people to say she's pale and thin, she's too happy about going to the farm to be cross with her mother and her aunt. After all, it's not the first time someone has mentioned these things. She gives Father one more hug and then runs to give Mother a quick kiss.

"I promise to be good," she tells Mother. "I won't go near the cows, and I'll be careful not to step on rusty nails or ruin my looks with freckles. And I'll eat lots of food and get big and fat like Rosa!"

"At least Anna can't skate at the farm," Aunt May says, reminding Mother of the day Anna skated down Bentalou Street, fell, and split her chin open.

"Why ever not?" Anna asks.

"No sidewalks in the country, *mein kleiner Zuckerwürfel*," Aunt May says. "No paved streets. Just dirt roads."

"Don't worry," Father says. "You'll find plenty of other things to do, Anna."

"That's just what worries me," says Mother. "Anna has too many notions in her head as it is. Without me to keep an eye on her, there's no telling what she'll think of."

Aunt May laughs. "Don't be silly, Lizzie. Anna has no more notions than any other healthy child."

Anna turns her head to hide a smile. Mother is right. Anna has many notions. But she has promised to be good and, even though it won't be easy, she will try to keep her word.

"When do I go to the farm?" she asks Father. "When? When?"

"Can you wait until after church tomorrow?" Father asks.

Mother gasps. "That soon?"

But Anna dances around the kitchen. "Hooray!" she shouts. "Hooray!"

"It has to be this week, Lizzie," Father tells Mother. "George begins harvesting the wheat next week."

"But I have to wash Anna's clothes, iron her dresses, darn her stockings—"

"Anna's going to the country, Lizzie," Aunt May says. "She doesn't need fancy clothing."

Mother frowns, but Father gives her a kiss. "May is right, Lizzie. Anna can wear her play clothes."

While Mother and Father talk, Anna runs to the parlor and peers out the front window. She's looking for Rosa and Beatrice, but she doesn't see them. Too bad. She can hardly wait to tell them that she, Anna, is going somewhere, after all.

◆ T W O ◆

Bears, Wolves, and Snakes

AFTER SUPPER, ANNA GOES OUTSIDE. CHARLIE IS sitting on his front steps, fanning his face with a comic book. Anna skips across the street to tell him her news.

"Guess what? Guess what?" Too excited to stand still, Anna hops back and forth from one foot to the other, waiting for Charlie to guess.

"What?" Charlie stares at her, his face puzzled. Behind him, his mother rocks a baby in her arms, trying to hush its cries. His little brothers race up and down the stairs. His older sister runs after them, begging them to hush before Papa gets cross and spanks them.

"I'm going to my Uncle George's farm tomorrow!" Anna cries. "I get to ride the train all by myself and stay for a whole week! I can wade in the pond and play in the barn, I can—"

Charlie fans his face harder. "Lucky you," he mutters.

Anna stops hopping and draws in her breath. Oh, no. Without meaning to, she's made Charlie feel just as bad as she felt when Rosa and Beatrice bragged about the ocean and the mountains. "I wish you were going, too," she tells him quickly. "It won't be any fun without you."

Charlie frowns and kicks a stone. He and Anna watch it bounce down the hill toward North Avenue. "Who wants to go to a dumb old farm?"

"I'll miss you, Charlie," Anna says.

Charlie doesn't answer. Instead, he sends another stone flying after the first one. It lands at the feet of the lamplighter, but he's too busy lighting the gas street-lamps to notice.

"At night it will be dark in the country," Charlie says. "Pitch-dark. No streetlights. There might be wild animals—bears and wolves. Poisonous snakes, too. Copperheads, water moccasins, rattlers."

Anna's heart beats a little faster. "I won't be scared," she says, "if that's what you're thinking."

"Your father won't be there to protect you," Charlie goes on. "You'll miss him and your mother so much I bet you'll cry yourself to sleep every night."

Anna's mouth feels dry. She's never spent a night away from Mother and Father. "I won't be homesick," she whispers, "if that's what you're thinking."

Charlie gets to his feet. "We'll see," he says.

Anna gets to her feet, too. "*I'll* see," she says, "not you. Because you won't be there to see anything!"

The two friends scowl at each other.

"I won't miss you one bit," Charlie says.

"I won't miss you, either!" Anna says.

"In fact, I'm glad you're leaving," Charlie says. "I wish you'd stay on the dumb old farm forever!"

"Maybe I will!" Anna sticks her nose up in the air and walks home. Behind her, she hears Charlie make a rude noise. What a stupid boy he is.

Father takes one look at Anna's face and asks, "Why, Anna, what's wrong?"

"I hate Charlie Murphy!" Anna wants to run to her room and cry, but the house has trapped every bit of the hot summer day upstairs.

Father takes her hand. "Did you and Charlie quarrel?"

Anna nods her head. "I told him I was going to the farm for a whole week, and he got mad. He said it will be dark in the country. Pitch-dark."

"There are no streetlights in the country," Father says, "but the moon and stars seem bigger and brighter there."

"Charlie said there'll be wild animals," Anna says.

"You'll see plenty of rabbits and squirrels," Father says. "You might see a raccoon, a possum, or maybe even a skunk."

"What about bears and wolves?"

Father laughs and shakes his head. "No bears, Anna. No wolves. Not in that part of Maryland, at least."

"No snakes, either?" Even though she's never seen one, Anna hates snakes more than anything in the world.

Father hesitates a moment. "I can't lie to you, Anna. You might see a snake or two, but most of them are harmless."

Anna shudders. She has no idea how to tell harm-

less snakes from harmful ones. Besides, in her opinion, no snakes are harmless.

She edges closer to Father. "Do you know what else Charlie said?"

Father shakes his head.

"He said I'll miss you and Mother," Anna whispers.

Father smiles. "We'll miss *you*, Anna."

Anna hugs Father. He smells like pipe tobacco and newspapers and shaving lotion. Charlie might have been wrong about the wild animals, but he was right about Father and Mother. She'll miss them very much.

Father points at the sky. "Look at the moon."

Anna tips her head back and stares at the moon's pale, lopsided face, looking down at her from high in the sky over the city.

"When you're at the farm," Father says, "think of Mother and me standing here on the sidewalk looking at the same moon you're looking at. Then you won't feel so far away."

Anna squeezes Father's hand as tightly as she can. "Me on the farm and you and Mother in Baltimore, all of us looking at the exact same moon at the exact same time." She likes that idea.

Father and Anna crook little fingers and solemnly promise to look at the moon every night just before Anna's bedtime.

"Now that we've settled that," Father says, "why don't you ask Charlie to walk down to the bakery with us? A nice big chocolate ice cream cone would cool you both off."

Anna's not sure Charlie wants to see her again. She's not sure she wants to see him, either. But she's leaving for the farm tomorrow. How can she go away and have fun if Charlie is mad at her? Besides, he loves ice cream even more than Anna does. He won't turn down a treat on a hot summer night.

Father pats the top of Anna's head. "Go on," he says.

Anna looks out the front door. It's dark now. All the neighbors have come outside to sit on their steps. Anna can smell Uncle Henry's cigar. She's glad Father smokes a pipe. It smells much nicer.

Uncle Henry says something and Aunt May laughs softly. Down on North Avenue, a streetcar clangs its bell. Up the street, Mrs. Schumaker sings to her baby. Mrs. Anderson's big collie barks. Aunt May's bulldog Fritzi answers with an even louder bark. Both Mrs. Anderson and Aunt May tell their dogs to be quiet.

Across the street, Mr. and Mrs. Murphy come outside to sit on their steps. The littlest Murphy cries. Charlie's sisters, Bridget and Molly, play hopscotch in the light from the streetlamp.

Anna sees Charlie standing in his doorway. He sees her, too. Slowly Anna crosses the street. Slowly, Charlie comes to meet her.

"Father and I are going to the bakery for ice cream," Anna says. "The honor of your company is requested."

Charlie laughs at Anna's fancy invitation and she laughs, too. Just like that, they are friends again.

At the bakery both Charlie and Anna pick chocolate ice cream. If Mother were with them, she'd make Anna choose vanilla. It doesn't stain clothes the way chocolate does.

"Eat it fast before it melts," Mr. Leidig says.

Father laughs. "You don't need to warn these two. That ice cream will disappear before you can say Jack Robinson!"

Anna, Charlie, and Father walk slowly home. It's too hot to hurry, too hot to talk, too hot to be angry.

◆ T H R E E ◆

"Good-bye, Baltimore!"

THAT NIGHT, ANNA LIES IN BED AND STARES AT THE skylight over her head. She can see a slice of moon and a few stars. *Der Mond und die Sterne,* Aunt May would say.

Anna wonders what it will be like to sleep in Aunt Aggie's house, far from home and Mother and Father. Suppose Father is wrong about the bears and the wolves? Suppose a snake slithers through her window and bites her while she's sleeping?

Maybe Anna shouldn't go away. Maybe she should stay right here in Baltimore and play with Charlie, as she always does. Thinking thoughts like this, Anna finally falls asleep.

After church the next day, Mother and Father take Anna to Camden Station. While they wait for the train, Anna begins to worry again. How will Father and Mother get along without her? How will she get along without them?

Just as Anna is about to say she's changed her mind, the station platform begins to shake under her feet. The train is coming. The locomotive huffs and puffs and screeches to a stop, belching clouds of steam. Cinders pepper Anna's pretty white dress. She smells hot grease and coal smoke. She moves closer to Father and puts her fingers in her ears to soften the sound of the whistle.

Passengers pour out of the cars. Friends and relatives rush to meet them. They hug and kiss and cry out their greetings.

The people who are leaving Baltimore begin to board the train. Anna hugs Father. She presses her face against his creamy white suit jacket to hide her tears. "Come with me, Father," she begs. "Come with me!"

Father frees himself gently. "I wish we could, but I

have to be at work bright and early tomorrow morning."

Mother smooths Anna's hair and brushes a speck of dust from her sleeve. "Mind your manners," she says. "And keep your face and hands clean. Remember you're a little lady, not a country bumpkin."

"Be sure and give Aggie and George our love," Father says. "And remember to look at the moon tonight."

Anna sniffs back her tears and tries to smile. She's nine years old, much too big to be a crybaby. "I'll look at the moon every single night," she promises.

Father and Mother kiss Anna. She hugs and kisses them. Mother tries to brush her tears away before Anna sees them. Father hands Anna her straw suitcase. Even though she still isn't sure she wants to go, she lets the conductor take the suitcase and help her up the steps and into the passenger car.

As the train pulls away, Anna waves at Mother and Father from the window until she can't see them anymore. Then she sits quietly in her seat and watches Baltimore disappear behind her. The houses get farther and farther apart. Yards grow bigger. There are more trees and fields.

Cinders blow in the open window. Motorcars and

horses wait at crossings for the train to thunder past. Anna waves. The drivers smile and wave back.

Soon the train slows for the first stop at Relay, then Elkridge, then Laurel. The conductor calls out the names of the towns. People get on and off, waving, hugging and kissing, rushing to greet each other on the station platforms.

The train is in the country now. Anna sees farms and woods, streams and dusty roads, a house here, a barn there, a store or two. A herd of cattle runs away from the train's whistle.

Just as Anna is beginning to enjoy the ride, the train stops at the Beltsville Station. The conductor helps Anna down the steps and hands her her suitcase. "Have a nice visit, young lady," he says.

Uncle George strolls toward Anna, tall and lanky in his faded overalls. "My, my," he exclaims. "Look at you, Anna! You've grown a foot since last Christmas. Why, you might catch up with me someday."

Uncle George is the tallest man Anna knows. Much taller than Aunt Aggie, much taller than Father. As much as Anna loves her uncle, she doesn't want to be as tall as he is.

"Where is Aunt Aggie?" Anna asks, looking around for her aunt.

"She's at home, making lemonade for you and me." Uncle George wipes his forehead with a bandana. "Whew, is it this hot in Baltimore?"

"It's even hotter," Anna says, lifting her arms to the breeze.

Uncle George tosses Anna's suitcase into the back of the farm wagon. Then he lifts Anna onto the high seat. His little dog, Jacko, wags his tail and licks Anna's hand.

Climbing up beside her, Uncle George slaps the reins against the horse's back. "Walk on, Alf," he says.

Alf pulls the wagon slowly over the dirt road, raising a cloud of dust that powders the weeds and wildflowers. Anna hears cicadas buzzing in the fields. A crow watches her from its perch on a fence post. Black-and-white cows gaze at her from a shady spot beside a stream. The air smells of fresh cut grass and honeysuckle. Anna smiles. Even Rehoboth Beach can't be better than this.

Uncle George's farm is high on a hill. Long before they get there, Anna sees the big white farmhouse, surrounded by Uncle George's fields. Rows of corn wave their silky tassels in the afternoon breeze, bending this way and that like waves in the ocean. The sound reminds Anna of waves, too, a gentle shushing song.

As soon as Aunt Aggie sees the wagon, she jumps up from her rocking chair on the porch and runs to meet Anna. Aunt Aggie is small and dark haired and thin, like Father and Anna.

"Anna!" Aunt Aggie cries, giving Anna a hug so hard it takes her breath away. "Don't you look pretty in that dress! Now, you come right inside and freshen up. You must be hot and thirsty and full of cinders."

While Anna washes her face and hands at the kitchen sink, Aunt Aggie pours her a tall glass of freshly squeezed lemonade. In Anna's opinion, Aunt Aggie makes the best lemonade in the world—not too sweet, not too sour, and the sugar is never gritty.

Suddenly, a boy a little taller than Anna comes to the back door and peers into the kitchen. "Is that the girl you said was coming?" he asks Aunt Aggie.

"Yes, Theodore," Aunt Aggie says. "This is my niece, Anna. Come inside and meet her properly."

Anna stares at Theodore's scowling face. His thick,

straight hair is so blond it's white. A towhead, Father would call him. His skin is tan, either from dirt or the sun—Anna isn't sure which. His overalls are faded and his bare feet are muddy. A country bumpkin, Mother would call him.

"Anna, this is Uncle George's nephew Theodore," Aunt Aggie says. "He's come to stay with us for a while."

Anna says hello, but her mouth is too stiff with dislike to smile. No one told her she'd have to share her aunt and uncle with a mean boy.

Theodore doesn't smile, either. It's clear he isn't any happier to see Anna than she is to see him.

"Father didn't tell me there was a boy living here," Anna says to Aunt Aggie.

Her aunt claps her hand to her forehead in dismay. "I do believe I forgot to tell Ira," she says. "I meant to, but the subject changed, and I never got around to it."

Aunt Aggie sighs. "Must mean I'm getting old and losing my memory." She pours a glass of lemonade for Theodore.

"Anna is my brother's daughter," she tells him. "You

two aren't really related, but I hope you'll think of each other as cousins."

Neither Anna nor Theodore says a word. Anna is glad Theodore isn't her real cousin. She'd hate to be related to a boy as rude and dirty as he is.

For a long time the only sound is the clink of ice cubes in Anna and Theodore's lemonade. When their glasses are empty, Aunt Aggie sends them outdoors to play.

The last time Anna visited, Uncle George made a swing for her in the big oak tree by the house. She runs toward it, but Theodore grabs the swing first. "City girl," he says. "Ain't you scared you'll get your pretty dress dirty?"

Anna sticks out her tongue. Theodore jumps from the swing, snatches Anna's fancy hair ribbon, and runs lickety-split across the yard.

Anna is furious. Charlie is the only boy who can steal Anna's ribbons and get away with it. She chases Theodore around the barn twice, but she cannot catch him.

Then Theodore scrambles up into an apple tree. He thinks he's safe, but Anna climbs after him. She doesn't stop, not even when her dress catches on a branch and tears. When she and Theodore can climb no higher, they glare at each other.

"Give me my bow," Anna says.

Theodore leans out of the tree and drops the bow. It flutters through the air like a big white butterfly and lands at the end of a branch where Anna cannot reach it.

"You're nothing but a stupid country bumpkin," Anna tells Theodore.

"You're nothing but a stuck-up city slicker," says Theodore.

"I am not!"

"You are, too!"

"Am not!"

"Are!"

Theodore clenches his fists as if he means to hit Anna. "Why don't you go back to Baltimore, where you belong?"

Anna makes the worst face she can think of. "Why don't you go back to your mother and father—or did they send you here to get rid of you?"

Theodore's face turns bright red and he takes a wild

swing at Anna. She backs away, catching her dress on another branch. Just as Theodore is about to shove Anna out of the tree, Aunt Aggie comes outside with a basket in her hand.

"Anna and Theodore," she calls, "come down from that tree and shell these peas for supper."

"Last one to the porch is a stuck-up city slicker!" Theodore yells.

Before Anna knows what he's up to, Theodore jumps out of the tree and runs across the grass. By the time Anna climbs down, Theodore is sitting on the porch sneering at her.

"City slicker," he whispers so Aunt Aggie won't hear.

But Aunt Aggie isn't paying any attention to Theodore. It's Anna she's staring at. "Oh, my word," Aunt Aggie says. "You haven't been here an hour and look at your dress. It's torn and dirty. What will your mother say?"

Anna swallows hard. Mother will be very cross. She spent hours making Anna's pretty lacy dress, and now it's ruined.

"And your hair ribbon," Aunt Aggie says. "What happened to it?"

Anna wants to say Theodore took it and threw it in the tree, but she hates tattletales. She hangs her head and says nothing. She wishes she were back home in Baltimore with all the other city slickers, sitting on the steps and sweating in the hot sun.

Aunt Aggie puts her hand on Anna's shoulder. "Come inside, Anna," she says softly. "I can wash and mend your dress so it will look as good as new."

Anna follows Aunt Aggie upstairs to the room where she always sleeps when she visits the farm. The wallpaper is printed with tiny blue flowers. The bed is made of carved oak. There's a matching bureau and washstand. In one corner is a big wardrobe. Aunt Aggie has already hung Anna's dresses there. On the table by the bed is a kerosene lamp with a pink glass shade. From the window, Anna can see Uncle George's rows of corn blowing in the breeze.

"What's a city slicker?" Anna asks her aunt.

"A city slicker?" Aunt Aggie laughs. "Why, that's a person from the big city who thinks country people are dumb."

"Am I a city slicker?" Anna asks.

"Of course not!" Aunt Aggie takes a long look at

Anna. "Did Theodore put that notion in your head?"

Anna toys with a strand of her hair. "I was just wondering," she says.

Aunt Aggie turns Anna around so she can unbutton the row of tiny buttons on the back of Anna's dress. "Such beautiful sewing," she says as she slips Anna's dress off. "I hope I can mend it properly."

Anna reaches for another dress, but Aunt Aggie shakes her head. "I have a better idea," she says. "I'll be back in a moment."

While she waits for her aunt to return, Anna leans on the window sill and looks out. Uncle George and his dog are coming up the dusty road. From here, he looks like a toy farmer in the garden under a Christmas tree.

"What do you think of these, Anna?" Aunt Aggie stands in the doorway holding up a pair of overalls, a shirt, and a straw hat. "They're too small for Theodore, but I bet they'd fit you just right!"

"But those are boys' clothes," Anna says.

Aunt Aggie shakes her head. "No reason a girl can't wear overalls." She winks at Anna. "Just think, you won't be tearing any more of those lovely dresses."

Slowly, Anna strips off her slip, fancy shoes, and hot stockings. When she's down to her drawers and camisole, she puts on the shirt, soft from many washings. Then she pulls on the overalls, stepping into each leg carefully. She feels very daring. Rosa and Beatrice would be shocked to see Anna in boys' clothes. Mother would have apoplexy.

Aunt Aggie shows Anna how to buckle the overall straps and hands her the straw hat.

"What about my shoes?" Anna asks.

"Shoes?" Aunt Aggie chuckles. "Pshaw, you don't need shoes in the country, Anna."

Anna studies her reflection in the wardrobe's mirrored door. Except for her long brown hair, she looks like a country boy. Anna grins at her new self, shoves her hands in her pockets, and follows Aunt Aggie downstairs. Before this week is over, Anna promises herself to show Theodore a thing or two about city slickers.

◆ F O U R ◆

The First Night Away

WHEN THEODORE SEES ANNA WEARING HIS OVER-
alls, he drops the peas he's shelling. "Those are mine,"
he says crossly.

Anna sits down beside him on the porch and begins
to shell peas. Her fingers shake a little. She's half afraid
Theodore might want his overalls back. "They're too
small for you," Anna says. "So Aunt Aggie gave them
to me. She said—"

"Girls shouldn't wear boys' clothes," Theodore
interrupts. "You look dumb and ugly in them."

Anna stares at Theodore's scowling face. No one has

ever called her dumb and ugly before. Not even Rosa. Her cheeks burn with anger and her eyes sting with tears. She's tempted to throw the whole bowl of peas at Theodore, but she knows Aunt Aggie would be cross if she did that.

Just as Anna opens her mouth to tell Theodore he's pretty dumb and ugly himself, Aunt Aggie looks out the kitchen door. "How are those peas coming?" she calls. "I need to cook them for supper."

For a while neither Anna nor Theodore says a word. The peas ping into Aunt Aggie's tin bowl. Chickens cluck as they scratch in the dust. Bees buzz in the hollyhocks growing beside the porch. Far away the train whistle blows.

Though Anna doesn't tell Theodore, she races him to see who can shell the fastest. She's pretty sure her fingers are quicker than his. But, then, maybe Theodore isn't racing.

After supper, everyone sits on the front porch and watches the sun set. It's lovely to see so much sky, Anna thinks. No tall buildings or chimneys block the view. The evening air is sweet with the smell of honeysuckle growing wild on the fence. A mockingbird sings in the pear tree.

As the light fades from the sky, Aunt Aggie points at the fireflies sparkling in the grass. "They look like tiny fairies carrying lanterns, flying about and searching for something they've lost," she says.

Anna looks at her aunt. "Do you believe in fairies?"

Theodore snorts, but Aunt Aggie shrugs. "When I was your age I believed in them."

"What about now?"

Uncle George chuckles. "There's no telling what odd notions Aggie has in that little head of hers."

Aunt Aggie pats Anna's hand. "I haven't seen a fairy yet," she admits, "but I don't totally discount the idea."

Anna leans back in her big rocking chair and smiles. "Me, neither," she says, prompting another snort from Theodore.

"Can I have a jar so I can catch me some fireflies?" he asks Aunt Aggie.

"Only if you promise to let them go before you come inside," Aunt Aggie says. Turning to Anna, she adds, "Would you like to catch fireflies, too?"

"I reckon she's scared of bugs," Theodore says. "Most girls are."

Anna remembers fireflies from other visits to the farm. She and Father caught a whole jarful last summer. "Ha," she says, "I bet I can catch more than you."

"We'll see about that," Theodore says.

Aunt Aggie goes inside and comes back with two Mason jars. "I punched holes in the lids when Anna was here last summer," she tells Theodore.

Anna runs across the lawn ahead of Theodore. The grass is already damp with dew. It feels delicious under her bare feet. She pulls up a handful of clover and drops it into her jar so the fireflies will feel at home.

Anna chases the fireflies and catches them carefully, snaring them in the air. She holds them in her hand for a moment, her fingers closed loosely around them, and enjoys the tickly feel of their feet on her palms. Then she drops them one by one into the jar until it's filled with twinkly fairy lights.

Nearby, Theodore fills his jar. Holding it up, he calls to Uncle George. "Who's got the most? Me or her?"

Uncle George squints hard. "They look exactly the same to me," he says.

Anna smiles. Even though she'd hoped Uncle George would say she'd caught more fireflies than Theodore, she knows Father would have said exactly the same thing.

"Let the poor things go now," Aunt Aggie calls, "and come to bed."

Anna hesitates. She wants to take the jar to her room. The fireflies would keep the night from being so dark. Shielding the jar to hide the light, she walks slowly toward the house.

"Hey," Theodore yells, "you can't take them inside. Didn't you hear what Aunt Aggie said?"

Anna notices Theodore hasn't freed his fireflies, either. "I'll let mine go when you let yours go," she says.

"I bet mine fly higher than yours," Theodore says.

Standing side by side, Anna and Theodore unscrew the tops from their jars. Out stream the fireflies, mixing with each other as they escape into the night. Neither Anna nor Theodore can tell whose fireflies fly higher.

Aunt Aggie calls again from the porch. Anna and Theodore race each other into the house. They reach

the door at the same time and bump into each other so hard they stumble into the hall.

Uncle George grabs the straps of Theodore's overalls and pulls him aside. "Where are your manners, Theodore?" he asks. "A gentleman always lets a lady go first."

Theodore scowls. "Anna ain't no lady," he mutters, "and I ain't no gentleman."

Uncle George shakes his head and leads Theodore to the pump for a good scrubbing. Aunt Aggie takes Anna's hand and they go upstairs together.

Anna washes her face and hands in a bowl of water on the nightstand. When she's ready for bed, Aunt Aggie says good night and tucks her under the sheet. "Sweet dreams," she whispers and blows out the kerosene lamp.

Anna watches her aunt leave the room. She listens to her go downstairs. Outside in the dark, leaves rustle and insects chirp.

No streetcars clang, no horses clip-clop past the house, no carts rattle, no motorcars chug-chug-chug up the hill, no footsteps pass beneath her window. Worst of all, Father and Mother are not sitting just outside on the front steps with Uncle Henry and Aunt May and Fritzi, the big white dog. Anna cannot hear Father's quiet chuckle or Uncle Henry's loud guffaw. She cannot hear Mother and Aunt May whispering secrets in German.

Then Anna remembers what she and Father promised to do. Quietly she slips out of bed and tiptoes to the window. The moon smiles down at her from high in the sky. Anna smiles back. At this very moment, far away in Baltimore, Father and Mother are looking at the exact same moon. They are thinking of Anna. They miss her just as much as she misses them.

Anna blows a kiss at the moon for Father and Mother. She imagines the moon carrying her kiss across the fields and woods, across the city rooftops, all the way to Anna's front steps on Warwick Avenue. It will fall down from the sky as softly as the first snowflake and land on Father's cheek.

Anna touches her own cheek to catch the kiss Father has just sent to her. Then she goes back to bed and snuggles under the covers. Soon Anna is fast asleep.

• F I V E •

Chores

WHEN ANNA COMES DOWNSTAIRS THE NEXT morning, Aunt Aggie has breakfast ready for her and Theodore. Pancakes with lots of syrup and bacon fried nice and crispy, just the way Anna likes it.

"Tell Anna what she has to do," says Theodore, talking with his mouth full of mushy pancakes. Syrup dribbles down his chin. Even though it's very early, his hands are already dirty.

Aunt Aggie gives Theodore a second helping of pancakes and offers more to Anna.

Anna shakes her head. "No, thank you," she says,

"I'm full." Although she doesn't ask, she wonders what Theodore wants her aunt to tell her.

"Tell her," Theodore says a little louder.

"Well," says Aunt Aggie with a smile, "I know you're a guest, Anna, but I'd like you to help Theodore do his chores. That way, you'll both be free to play when you're finished."

Too surprised to say anything, Anna stares at her aunt. Help Theodore? Anna has never heard such a terrible idea. Besides, she doesn't want to play with him.

"It's the fair thing to do," Theodore says. "If I have to work, you should, too."

"But I don't know anything about farms," Anna says. "How can I do chores?"

"City slicker," Theodore hisses.

Aunt Aggie frowns at Theodore. "Now, now, I won't have you calling each other names."

Turning to Anna, she says, "The first thing Theodore does every morning is feed the chickens and gather their eggs. You can do that."

That doesn't sound too bad. Chickens are soft and feathery, nothing to be afraid of. But what if they don't like people to take their eggs?

43

After breakfast, Anna follows Theodore outside. The chickens live in a little whitewashed shed inside a wire fence. Three or four brown hens peck in the dirt, clucking to themselves. They have long yellow legs and big feet with sharp toenails. They tilt their heads and stare at Anna with beady eyes. They do not look as friendly as Anna had hoped.

Theodore opens the gate and goes inside, but Anna hesitates. She's used to pigeons but not birds the size of these.

Theodore grins. "Scaredy cat."

"I am not." Anna steps into the chickens' yard, and Theodore hands her a bucket of feed.

"Scatter it on the ground," he says.

The chickens scurry around Anna's feet pecking at the grain. She wishes she'd put on her shoes. What if the hens mistake her toes for food? Their beaks are so sharp. And their eyes are so wicked.

"Go inside the coop and get the eggs while the chickens are eating," Theodore says. "And don't break any."

Anna picks up the basket by the door and goes inside the hen house. She wrinkles her nose. Chickens smell worse than pigeons.

Just as Anna reaches for an egg, she hears a loud rustling sound in a dark corner. Before she understands what's happening, a huge bird flies at her, wings flapping. Its beak is sharp and pointed. It has claws.

Anna screams and throws the egg basket at the bird. She runs toward the door, but it slams shut in her face. Above the cackle of the bird, she hears Theodore laughing.

"Let me out!" Anna shrieks, but Theodore leans against the door and holds it shut. The bird flies at Anna's head. She covers her face with her hands, sure the bird will peck out her eyes. She feels its wings beat against her, she feels its claws and its beak.

"Aunt Aggie!" Anna cries. "Uncle George! Help, help!"

Suddenly, Anna hears a shout. The door flies open and Aunt Aggie rushes into the chicken coop. She hurls a bucket of water at the bird.

"You ornery old critter!" Aunt Aggie yells. "I swear I'd cook you for Sunday dinner if you weren't so tough!"

The rooster flies up to a rafter and crows.

"Don't be so sure of yourself," Aunt Aggie tells him. "There's always the stew pot!"

Anna runs out of the chicken coop. The hens look

up from the dirt and regard her with their wicked eyes. Theodore is nowhere in sight.

Aunt Aggie puts her arm around Anna. "I should have warned you about the rooster, but I didn't dream Theodore would play such a mean trick on you. Just wait till I get my hands on that rascal!"

Anna tries to stop crying. "Are you going to spank him?" she asks.

Aunt Aggie scowls. "Why, I suppose I'll leave that up to George."

Anna brushes away her tears. Although she has never had a paddling herself, she's sure that's just what Theodore deserves.

"Come inside and sit a spell," Aunt Aggie says. "You look plum tuckered out."

When Uncle George comes home for noontime dinner, Anna is sitting on the front porch with Aunt Aggie, sipping a glass of lemonade. By now she's almost forgotten her encounter with the rooster, but Aunt Aggie hasn't.

"Theodore locked Anna in the chicken coop with the rooster," she tells Uncle George. "I think you should give him a spanking."

Uncle George wipes the sweat off his forehead and takes a glass of lemonade from Aunt Aggie. "You want me to spank the rooster?"

Anna giggles, but Aunt Aggie looks cross. "You know perfectly well what I mean, George Armiger. Theodore treated Anna very badly. That rooster scared the poor child half to death."

Uncle George looks around. "Where is Theodore?" he asks.

"I haven't seen hide nor hair of him all morning," Aunt Aggie says. "Which means he never finished his chores. The garden hasn't been weeded or watered and the eggs haven't been collected."

Uncle George sighs and sips his lemonade. When he is finished, he hands the empty glass to Aunt Aggie and walks to the porch railing.

"Theodore!" he shouts. "You come here this minute!"

Uncle George's voice is so loud it echoes from the side of the barn, but Theodore does not appear.

Uncle George calls again, even louder this time. The chickens pecking in the yard look up and squawk. Uncle George's dog barks. A crow caws. The rooster crows.

Finally, Theodore comes creeping out from behind the barn. When he reaches the porch steps, Uncle George grabs his overall straps and lifts Theodore clear off the ground.

"What is this about the rooster?" he bellows in Theodore's face. "You frightened Anna! Is that the proper way to treat a guest?"

Giving Theodore a little shake, Uncle George whacks him on the rear end with his big hand. Clap! Theodore winces. Anna winces, too. Maybe it would have been better to spank the rooster, after all.

"Tell Anna you're sorry," Uncle George orders.

Theodore hesitates. Uncle George raises his hand again. Without meeting Anna's eyes, Theodore quickly says, "I'm sorry."

He doesn't sound sorry and he doesn't look sorry, but no one notices this except Anna.

"Where's my dinner, Aggie?" Uncle George asks. "I'm starved. Spanking a child is mighty hard work."

After a big meal of corn and ham, Uncle George leans across the table and stares hard at Theodore. "From now on, you'll do your chores by yourself. Anna is our guest. She doesn't have to help you."

Anna can't help smiling at Theodore. He kicks her under the table. Anna opens her mouth to tell Uncle George, but Theodore gives her such a wicked look she takes another bite of her biscuit instead. There's no telling what Theodore might do the next time she's alone with him.

Getting Even

THAT AFTERNOON, ANNA SITS DOWN IN THE SHADE of a big tree with a book she brought from home, but instead of reading, she watches Theodore work in the garden. The sun beats down on his blond hair. It beats down on the tomato plants and the marigolds. It beats down on the beans and the squash. Theodore looks hot and tired and grumpy.

It serves him right, Anna thinks.

Theodore turns his head and catches Anna watching him. He makes a face even uglier than his natural everyday ugly face. Anna sticks out her tongue and makes a rude noise. At the same time she bunches her legs under her, ready to jump up and run if she has to.

But Theodore spits in the dust and turns his back on Anna. For some reason, this makes Anna even madder than the face he made. She wants to get even with him for locking her in the chicken coop with the rooster, but she can't think of what to do. That's when she notices the watering can Theodore has been using. What if she sneaks up behind him and pours water on his head?

Anna presses her hand to her mouth to keep from giggling. She's never done anything quite so bad, but even if Uncle George spanks her for it, Anna doesn't care. She wants to play a trick on Theodore. He deserves it.

While Theodore bends over the weeds, Anna tip-toes across the grass and picks up the watering can. Holding her breath, she creeps as close as she dares and lifts the watering can high. Out of the spout comes a shower of water that drenches Theodore's hair and overalls. He lets out a roar of anger, but Anna is already running as fast as she can toward the house.

She dashes inside well ahead of him and slams the

screen door in his face. Then she scoots behind Aunt Aggie, who is stirring a pot on the stove.

Aunt Aggie stops stirring and stares at Theodore. "Stay where you are," she says, stopping him on the threshold. "You're all wet. Don't you dare put one muddy foot on my clean kitchen floor."

"Anna dumped water on me!" Theodore yells. His face is red with either anger or sunburn. Anna can't tell which.

Aunt Aggie turns to Anna, but before her aunt can ask any questions, Anna says, "Poor Theodore was so hot. I thought the water would cool him off." It's hard for Anna to speak without laughing.

Aunt Aggie frowns. "Do you think I was born yesterday, Anna Sherwood?"

Now Anna's face turns red. "I was just trying to be nice," she fibs, still hoping to stay out of trouble.

"I don't believe that," Aunt Aggie says sharply.

"It's Theodore's fault," Anna mutters, feeling sulky. "He started it when he shut me in the chicken coop with that rooster."

Theodore scowls at Anna through the screen door. Turning her head to hide her face from Aunt Aggie,

Anna crosses her eyes and sticks out her tongue. Theodore makes an even worse face.

"Shame on you, Theodore," Aunt Aggie says. "Suppose your face freezes like that?"

"Suppose hers does?" Theodore points at Anna.

Aunt Aggie looks at Anna. "Did you make a face at Theodore?"

Anna fidgets with her overall straps. Theodore is ruining her vacation. He's worse than Rosa.

"Why does Theodore have to be here?" she wails.

Before Aunt Aggie can stop her, Anna runs upstairs to her hot room and slams the door. She throws herself on her bed and cries.

A few minutes later, Aunt Aggie opens the door and sits down on the bed beside Anna.

"I want to go home," Anna sobs.

"Now, now," Aunt Aggie says, stroking Anna's long hair. "You've only been here a day. Why don't you try to stick it out till Sunday?"

To Anna, Sunday is years and years away. She'll be an old lady by the time it comes. Her hair will be white, and she'll walk with a cane like Rosa's grandmother. "I want to leave now," she insists.

"But the church supper and dance is Saturday night," Aunt Aggie says. "Surely you don't want to miss that!"

Anna takes a deep breath and sees visions of crispy fried chicken, corn on the cob dripping with butter, all the iced tea she can drink, baked beans, cole slaw, sweet green pickles, soft rolls, homemade ice cream, chocolate cake, blueberry pie. Anna's mouth waters so much her jaws ache.

"Are you going to make your special potato salad?" she asks her aunt.

"I most certainly am!" Aunt Aggie gives Anna a hug. "I might even bake a fresh peach cobbler."

Anna hesitates. Potato salad and peach cobbler are two of her very favorite foods. "Will Theodore still be here?" she asks slowly, hoping, hoping, hoping her aunt will say no.

Aunt Aggie nods. "Yes, he will."

Anna makes a face without meaning to. "I thought his mother and father might be coming to get him soon."

"Anna," Aunt Aggie says quietly, "there's something you should know about Theodore."

"I already know all I want to know about him," Anna says. Taking a deep breath, she adds, "He's mean, and I hate him."

When Aunt Aggie sighs, Anna feels bad. "Theodore hates me, too," she says quickly. "That's why he shut me in the chicken coop and stole my ribbon and made me rip my dress and called me a city slicker."

"Theodore has had a difficult time lately," Aunt Aggie says slowly. "Things have been hard for him."

Aunt Aggie pauses. The room is so quiet Anna can hear a bee buzzing against the window screen.

"Theodore's an orphan," Aunt Aggie says at last. "That's why he's staying with us. Uncle George is his guardian."

Shocked, Anna draws in her breath so hard she almost chokes. "Theodore's mother and father are dead?"

Aunt Aggie nods. A breeze stirs the hot air, bringing the smell of roses through the open window.

Anna slides closer to her aunt. She doesn't want to think about losing her father or her mother, but if something did happen to them, she'd be mad, too.

Mad enough to lock someone in a chicken coop. Mad enough to make faces. Mad enough to be rude.

"What happened to them?" Anna whispers.

"His father caught pneumonia and died two years back," Aunt Aggie says. "And his mother—well, she never was a strong woman. She died of a fever in the spring."

Aunt Aggie takes Anna's face between her two small hands and peers deeply into her eyes. "Promise to be patient with Theodore," she says. "The child is hurting something awful."

Anna promises. But it won't be easy. Even though she feels sorry for Theodore, she doesn't like him. Anna supposes she must be a very hardhearted girl. The heroines in her books would forgive Theodore at once and be endlessly kind to him. Elsie Dinsmore, for instance. Or Pollyanna. Too bad Anna isn't more like them.

After a while, Aunt Aggie pats Anna's hand. "Would you like to cool off in the farm pond?"

"How can I go in the water? I didn't bring my bathing costume," Anna says sadly.

"Oh, for goodness sake," Aunt Aggie says. "We're

not going to a public beach. You can wear your drawers."

"Go outside in my underwear?" Anna stares at her aunt, truly shocked. "What will people think?"

Aunt Aggie laughs. "You silly goose. Who will see you?"

"Theodore," Anna mutters.

"He'll have his drawers on, too," Aunt Aggie says.

Suddenly, Anna feels very daring. Hasn't she been wearing overalls for two days and going barefoot and doing all sorts of unladylike things? Why not go swimming in her drawers? On a hot day like this, it would be fun to play in the farm pond.

"Promise you won't tell Mother," Anna begs.

Aunt Aggie promises. Lifting a long strand of Anna's hair, she says, "Suppose we braid this to keep it out of your face?"

Anna bites her lip. "Mother never braids my hair. She says my face is too long and narrow and my ears stick out. I'd look ugly."

"Fiddle faddle." Aunt Aggie takes Anna down the hall to her room and divides Anna's hair into two neat braids. When she's finished, she ties the ends with yarn from her sewing basket and leads Anna to a mirror. "There," she says. "You see? You aren't a bit ugly."

Anna studies her reflection. No matter what Aunt Aggie says, Mother is right. Her ears stick out and her face is long and narrow. To be pretty, Anna should be pink-cheeked and plump, not pale and thin. Her hair should be blond and curly, not brown and straight. She should look like Rosa. Mother is always praising Rosa's blond curls and plump little hands, her bright blue eyes and her dimples. Just thinking about Rosa makes Anna grit her teeth.

While Anna stands there staring at herself, she feels a breeze on the back of her neck. She shakes her head and watches her braids fly out like long brown ropes. No more thick hot hair hanging down her back, no more ribbons to lose, no more tangles. Anna feels cooler already.

She studies herself in the mirror again, turning this way and that to admire her braids. They aren't blond and the ends don't curl, but Anna likes the way they feel. When she goes back to Baltimore, she plans to wear her hair in braids every day except Sunday. Even if she has to learn to do it herself. Even if her face is long and narrow. Even if her ears stick out. Even if Mother thinks she looks ugly.

Turning away from the mirror, she hugs her aunt, who is just as pale and thin as she is.

"Now, go get ready to take a swim," Aunt Aggie says.

◆ S E V E N ◆

Mud Monsters

*A*NNA GOES BACK TO HER ROOM AND PULLS A union suit out of the bureau. Although she hadn't wanted to bring it, Anna is glad Mother insisted she'd need it if the weather turned cold. Except for the buttons up the front and the flap in the back, the union suit looks very much like a bathing costume. Maybe Theodore won't notice it's really her underwear.

Anna runs outside, feeling very daring. If Mother saw her, she'd send her to her room for the rest of her life. She'd tell Aunt May that Anna was a disgrace. But Aunt May would just laugh. That would make Mother so cross she'd go home in a huff and refuse to speak to her sister for a week.

Theodore is already in the pond when Anna arrives. She walks out to the end of the little wooden dock Uncle George built and watches him. He's floating on his back with his eyes closed. If he weren't an orphan, Anna would sneak up on him and duck him. But she's promised Aunt Aggie to be nice.

Anna sits down on the end of the dock and dangles her feet in the water. It feels cool. She wants to jump in before Theodore sees her underwear, but she's just a little bit afraid of the pond. Suppose the bottom is muddy? Suppose there are fish that bite? Suppose there are snakes?

Anna glances behind her. Aunt Aggie is sitting on the porch, keeping an eye on the children. Maybe she should go and ask her aunt about mud and fish and snakes and other dangerous things she hasn't even thought of.

At that moment, Theodore opens his eyes and sees Anna. He starts to laugh. "I see Paris, I see France," he calls, "I see someone's underpants!"

Anna feels her face turn bright red. She wants to turn around and run to her room and never come out, but instead she yells, "This is my bathing costume, you big dummy! In Baltimore, it's the latest style!"

Theodore hoots. "I know underwear when I see it!"

Anna is so mad she forgets about the mud and the fish that bite and the snakes. Planning to splash Theodore, she flings herself into the water and sinks into the mud on the bottom.

Anna comes up spluttering. "Oooooh," she screams. "Oooooh!" The mud is slimy and it feels horrible. She slogs toward the shore, screeching, and Theodore chases her, splashing water all over her.

Anna turns around to splash him and gets a face full of water. Without thinking, she bends down and scoops up two handfuls of black gooey mud. She throws them both at Theodore, hitting him right in the face.

He throws mud at Anna. She throws more mud at him. The mud flies back and forth.

"Stop it, Theodore!" Aunt Aggie cries from the dock. "Stop it, Anna!"

The two of them stop and stare at each other. They are both streaked and smeared with mud. It coats their skin and cakes their hair. Anna has never been so dirty in her whole entire life.

Safe and dry on the dock, Aunt Aggie begins to laugh. "All you two need is feathers," she says. "You've already been tarred!"

Theodore looks at Anna. He laughs, too. "You should see yourself," he says. "Your own mother wouldn't know you!"

Anna can't help giggling. Mother would be horrified but not so horrified she wouldn't recognize Anna. Running past Theodore, Anna throws herself face down in the pond and flops around like a fish, swishing herself clean.

When she stands up, she sees Theodore rubbing more mud into his hair. Waving his arms, he prances through the water, roaring, "Look at me, Aunt Aggie! I'm a monster!"

Anna scoops up handfuls of mud. Like Theodore, she rubs it all over herself. "I'm a monster, too!" she shouts. "Look at me, Aunt Aggie! Look!"

Anna throws back her head and howls. She waves her arms. She jumps up and down. She chases Theodore. She ducks him. He ducks her. They splutter and laugh and choke on the pond water.

Aunt Aggie calls Uncle George to come and watch.

They stand together on the dock and laugh at the monsters.

Anna can't remember ever having so much fun.

By the time the two of them leave the pond, Anna decides Theodore isn't as awful as she thought. When she glances at him, he grins and tugs one of her braids, but not hard enough to hurt.

"You aren't half bad for a girl," he says and runs off.

Pleased, Anna saunters into the house. Her wet braids thwack her back as she runs upstairs to wash the last of the mud away. Just as she finishes drying her face, she hears Theodore howling in protest. Anna pokes her head out the bedroom window. In the yard below, Uncle George is scrubbing Theodore under the pump.

Anna laughs to herself and pulls on her overalls. A good scrubbing certainly won't hurt Theodore.

After supper, Theodore and Anna sit on the porch steps. It's a hazy night, still hot after the long sunny day. The honeysuckle on the fence glitters with fireflies, but Anna and Theodore are too lazy to catch them.

Behind them, Aunt Aggie and Uncle George talk softly. Their rocking chairs squeak. Jacko scratches fleas. His leg thumps the porch. Somewhere in the dark, a mockingbird sings. Crickets chirp.

"It's so quiet here," Anna says softly.

Theodore nods. "I guess there's a lot of racket in Baltimore. Cars, trains, trolleys. It's a wonder folks can sleep at night."

"You get used to it," Anna says, suddenly feeling homesick for city sounds.

"Not me," Theodore says. "I'm going to be a farmer all my life, just like Uncle George."

"I intend to travel and see the world," Anna says. "The pyramids in Egypt, the Roman Coliseum, the Leaning Tower of Pisa, the Eiffel Tower, Buckingham Palace." As she names the places she plans to see, Anna pictures them as they appeared in her world geography book, drawn carefully in black ink. Someday she'll see them in full color.

"You better marry a millionaire," Theodore says.

Anna sighs. She doesn't know any millionaires and has no idea how she'd ever meet one.

"I'm saving the money myself," she says. "Every

time someone gives me a dime or a nickel, I put it in a special jar. When I'm grown up, I'll have at least a hundred dollars."

"If I had a hundred dollars, I'd buy a farm," Theodore says.

Anna gazes at the moon just swinging up from behind the trees. She thinks of Father and Mother sitting on the steps on Warwick Avenue, looking at the same moon she's looking at. If she goes to Egypt or Rome, Paris or London, the moon will be there, too. It will shine down on her in foreign lands and on Father and Mother in Baltimore and on Theodore in Beltsville. Even though they will be far apart, the moon will keep them together.

◆ E I G H T ◆

Cousin Herman

N͟ext morning, Aunt Aggie finds chores for Anna to do inside while Theodore works outside. First Anna washes the breakfast dishes, and then she helps her aunt make peach preserves. It's a hot job, but Aunt Aggie promises Anna she will give her three jars to take home with her.

"Each time you spread peach preserves on your breakfast toast, you'll remember your week on the farm," Aunt Aggie says.

When all the peaches are sealed up in Mason jars with tight lids, Aunt Aggie tells Anna she needs a few things from Mr. Buell's Store—a pound of sugar, a half pound of coffee, a pound of flour, and six lemons. She gives Anna a list and two dollars.

"Take Theodore with you," Aunt Aggie says. "There should be enough left over to treat yourselves to peppermint sticks or licorice."

Anna slips the money into her overall pocket and runs outside to find Theodore. He has just finished weeding the garden.

"Aunt Aggie wants us to go to the store," Anna tells him. "We can get candy with the change."

Theodore grins and throws down the hoe. The two of them set off down the lane to the road.

After a few minutes, Anna gets a funny idea. She takes off her hat. Holding her braids on top of her head, she puts the hat back on. "Let's play a trick on Mr. Buell," she tells Theodore. "Let's pretend I'm a boy."

Theodore studies Anna. "He'll never believe that," he says. "You walk like a girl."

"Show me how *you* walk," Anna says. "And I'll copy you."

Theodore swaggers down the dusty road ahead of

Anna, his hands in his pockets. Anna watches him carefully. Shoving her hands in her pockets, she strides after him, taking big steps and bouncing along on her bare feet in a way that would scandalize Mother. By the time they reach Mr. Buell's Store, Anna is sure she's walking just like a boy. Why, she'd probably fool her own father and mother.

Theodore stops on the store's front steps. "What am I supposed to call you?" he asks Anna.

"Herman," Anna says, thinking of one of her German cousins. "Tell Mr. Buell my name is Herman and I'm Aunt Aggie's nephew from Germany."

"Mr. Buell knows your aunt's got no kin in Germany," Theodore says.

"Say I'm a long-lost relative," Anna says, warming to her story. "Say my father is Aunt Aggie's cousin once or twice removed. He went off to Germany and married a duchess, and Aunt Aggie never knew what became of him till now."

"That's plain silly." Theodore spits in the dirt, just missing Anna's big toe. "Mr. Buell will never believe it."

"Just tell him, Theodore!" Anna feels cross. "Don't you have any imagination?"

Theodore shrugs. "Oh, all right. Being from Germany might explain why you're so peculiar."

Anna spits in the dirt, just missing Theodore's big toe. Then she follows him into the store, keeping her hands in her pockets and remembering to swagger.

After the bright sunlight, it's dark inside, but Anna can see long strips of flypaper hanging from the ceiling, twirling in the breeze from the fan. She breathes in the musty odor of chicken feed mixed in with the smells of cheese and kerosene and floor wax.

Farm tools, overalls, and rubber boots hang from the ceiling, and the shelves are jammed with just about everything a person might need, from bolts of fabric to lamp oil, tools, and canned goods. The hodgepodge is very different from city stores that sell special things: food in one shop, clothing in another, hardware some-place else, and so on.

Mr. Buell is chatting with two men at the counter. When he sees Theodore and Anna, he smiles.

"Well, well, Theodore, what can I do for you today?" he asks.

Theodore takes the list from Anna and thrusts it across the counter. "Aunt Aggie needs these things."

Mr. Buell glances at the list and nods. Then he turns his attention to Anna. "Aren't you going to introduce me to your friend, Theodore? I don't recollect seeing him around here before."

Anna grins. Mr. Buell has just said "him." So far, so good. He thinks she's a boy.

Theodore takes a deep breath. "This here is Herman, Aunt Aggie's long-lost relative from Germany. His daddy ran off with a Dutch lady and now he's here for a visit."

"You don't say." Mr. Buell leans across the counter and peers at Anna's face. "I didn't know Aggie had relatives overseas."

"*Guten tag,*" Anna says politely, trying to remember the German she's learned from Mother.

"Good day, to you, too," says Mr. Buell.

Switching to English, Anna imitates her grandfather's accent. "*Ich* been pleased to meet you."

Mr. Buell chuckles. "*Sehr angenehm,*" he says. "Pleased to meet you, too!"

Anna's face turns red. She hadn't expected Mr. Buell to know German.

"Where are you from?" he asks. "What city?"

"Hanover," Anna says, glad she can remember where Grandfather was born.

"Ah, I know Hanover well," Mr. Buell says. "What street do you live on?"

Anna's face turns redder. Why did she start this silly game? "*Ich* forgetten," she stammers, still trying to sound German.

Theodore rises on his toes to look Mr. Buell in the eye. "Can you please give us what Aunt Aggie needs?" he asks. "She wants to make lemonade for Uncle George. It has to be ready by noon, so we're in a hurry."

"Sure, sure." Mr. Buell winks at the other men. "It's not often I meet someone from my native land, you know. Such a handsome young lad. Almost too pretty to be a boy."

Anna stares at the floor. She will never set foot inside this store again.

Whistling a tune, Mr. Buell fills a bag with sacks of sugar, coffee, and flour and drops in six lemons. "That will be one dollar and three cents," he says.

Anna pulls the money out of her pocket and slaps it down on the counter. "Vee vant two peppermint sticks," she says, still trying. "*Und* some licorice, *bitte.*"

"Ah, I like children who say *please.*" Mr. Buell drops a handful of peppermint sticks into the bag and adds a handful of stringy black licorice. Handing the bag to Anna, he says, "Here you are Herman," he says. "Your candy and your change."

"Danke schön," Anna says, dropping ninety cents into her pocket.

"You are very welcome, indeed," Mr. Buell tells Anna. Turning to Theodore, he says, "If you see your aunt's niece Anna, be sure and say hello for me. I thought she was visiting this week, but I must have been mistaken."

Theodore gives Anna a push. "Let's go. Aunt Aggie needs these things right away."

"Auf Wiedersehen," Mr. Buell calls as Anna and Theodore leave the store.

Outside in the sunlight, Theodore glares at Anna. "I never felt like such a moron in my whole life!"

Anna scowls at Theodore. "It's all your fault. You should have told me Mr. Buell was German."

"I wish you really were a boy," Theodore says, "so I could punch you in the nose."

"Go ahead! Punch me!" Anna sets the grocery bag

on the ground and doubles her fists. She's seen boys fight. She's sure she knows how to do it. "I'll punch you right back!"

Theodore makes a fist and punches Anna in the chin but not very hard. She punches him. He punches her a little harder. Anna's hat flies off. Her braids tumble down her back. Theodore grabs one and pulls. Anna screeches.

Suddenly, Mr. Buell is between them. "Children, children!" With one hand he grabs Theodore. With the other he grabs Anna. He holds the two of them apart and looks at them.

"My, my," he says. "Just look at Herman's braids. Is this how boys in Germany wear their hair nowadays?"

Theodore starts to laugh. Even though she's embarrassed, Anna laughs, too.

Mr. Buell chuckles. "It seems you rascals tried to play a trick on me."

"It was all Anna's idea," Theodore says. "I told her you'd never believe her, but she just had to go and act the fool."

Anna stops laughing. If Mr. Buell weren't still holding her arm, she'd punch Theodore for calling her a fool.

"Oh, but I did believe Anna," Mr. Buell says. "I never would have given you all that candy if I hadn't been so happy to see such a nice little boy from my native land."

Anna feels happy again. "I'm not a fool, after all," she tells Theodore, leaning around Mr. Buell to see him better. "You have me to thank for the extra candy."

"You have Anna to thank for this, too." Mr. Buell pulls two cold bottles of sarsaparilla out of a tub full of ice and water. "There you are," he says, handing them each one. "No more fighting, okay?"

Anna looks at Theodore. Theodore looks at Anna. They grin. A hot sunny day, two bottles of sarsaparilla, and all the candy they can eat. Being friends is definitely more fun than being enemies. At least for right now.

NINE

Princess Nell

*T*HAT AFTERNOON, AUNT AGGIE SENDS THEODORE and Anna down to the end of the lane to wait for the mailman. It's about time for the Sears and Roebuck catalog to come. Aunt Aggie's been wanting one of the new gas ranges they sell. She's hoping this year Uncle George will say they can afford it.

"It will be a long wait," Theodore tells Anna. "Mr. O'Reilly stops and talks to everybody. He tells who got letters from far away, who had a death in the family, who had a marriage, who had a baptizing. He knows everything there is to know about all the folks in Beltsville."

Anna wonders if girls are allowed to be mailmen. Think of all the postcards she could read. Why, she'd learn all about the world and everyone in it. It's the most perfect job she can think of.

"I bet Mr. O'Reilly's told everybody in Beltsville you're here," Theodore adds.

Anna smiles. If Theodore is right, she's famous, at least in Beltsville. She wants to hear more of Mr. O'Reilly's gossip, but Uncle George calls Theodore to hoe the tomato patch.

Theodore makes a face Uncle George can't see. Anna knows he hates to hoe in the hot sun. "Tell me if the catalog comes," he tells Anna. Then he heads up the lane to meet Uncle George.

Left alone, Anna climbs on the fence and leans over so she can see way down the road. In the city, the streets would be full of people coming and going. But here there's not a person in sight, not a car, not even a horse pulling a wagon. Birds sing, a rabbit runs across the road, butterflies drift from one clump of wildflowers to the next, cicadas rasp in the tall grass. The air smells sweet.

Anna sits on the top rail of the fence, making a

clover chain and whistling songs she learned in school, "The Battle Hymn of the Republic," "Maryland, My Maryland," "Oh, Susanna." She's glad Mother can't hear her. According to Mother, it's unladylike to whistle. Sometimes Anna thinks everything that's fun is unladylike. Going barefoot, wearing overalls, swimming in your drawers, getting dirty, whistling, spitting. Boys don't know how lucky they are.

At last, Anna sees someone coming, but it's not Mr. O'Reilly. It's a girl riding a horse. She's at least fifteen, much older than Anna, and very pretty. She wears jodhpurs and tall, shiny riding boots and a smart velvet jacket. Her long golden hair waves around her face and down over her shoulders. Her horse is slim legged and graceful. Its mane is braided, and so is its tail. Head up, it trots along, lifting its hooves high, as if it doesn't like the feel of the ground.

To Anna's delight, the girl slows to a stop and smiles at her.

"You must be Mrs. Armiger's niece Anna," the girl says. "All the way from Baltimore."

"How did you know?" Anna asks. "Has Mr. O'Reilly been to your house already?"

The girl laughs, showing the most perfect teeth Anna has ever seen. "My mother told me you were here. She and your aunt are friends."

Leaning closer, the girl says, "My name's Nell Webster. I live on the farm next to your aunt and uncle. Do you like horses?"

Anna nods. She loves horses. In fact, she's dying to pet Nell's horse, but Father has taught her never to touch the horses she sees in the city. They are work horses, he says. They aren't meant for petting.

"His name is Silver Heels." Nell reaches into her pocket, pulls out a slice of apple, and hands it to Anna. "Feed him that and he'll love you forever."

Silver Heels leans toward Anna. His warm breath tickles her hand as he gently takes the apple from her outstretched palm. Anna giggles. "Is it all right to pet him?" she asks.

"Of course." Nell smiles at Anna. "Silver Heels is very spoiled. He expects to be petted."

Anna gently strokes Silver Heels' long velvety face. He makes a whuffing sound and she feels his warm breath again. "He's the most beautiful horse I've ever seen," she whispers.

"Would you like to go for a ride?" Nell asks.

Anna is almost too amazed at her good luck to say yes. Before she can pinch herself to see if she's dreaming, she's perched on the horse, in front of Nell.

Nell nudges Silver Heels and says, "Let's go, fellow."

Anna sits tall and proud. She can see over the fields of corn, down the hill to the woods beyond. Far away Uncle George is working in the tomato patch. Theodore trudges along behind him. Anna feels sorry for him. She hopes Nell will take Theodore for a ride some other time.

"Let's go a little faster," Nell says.

Anna holds Silver Heels' mane. He picks up speed. The gentle rolling motion of his walk changes. He trots, bouncing Anna up and down. The summer air feels cooler as it rushes against her face. She wishes they could go even faster.

After a few minutes, they come to a low point in the road. On either side, the trees lean toward each other as if they're holding hands to make an arch. They cast deep green shadows on the road. Anna sees a bridge ahead.

"Silver Heels needs a drink," Nell says. She slides

down from the horse, but she tells Anna to stay in the saddle. "I'll lead him to the creek."

Nell guides Silver Heels off the road and along a mossy path. Honeysuckle drapes a fence and wild grape hangs from the trees. Sunlight dapples the leaves with gold. It splashes down on Nell and Silver Heels, too, making patterns everywhere.

Anna hears the stream before she sees it. The water is shallow, but it races over stones, making a loud chatter. While Silver Heels drinks, Anna pretends she and Nell are princesses in a magic land. She can almost see fairies hiding in the leaves. She can almost hear them laughing.

Nell sits on the bank and pulls off her tall boots. "My feet are so hot," she says. "Let's wade in the stream."

Nell helps Anna down from Silver Heels' back, and the two girls splash into the cold water. The stones are slippery with moss. Suddenly, Anna's feet slide out from under her and she lands with a big splash in the middle of the creek. For a moment, Anna is too surprised to move. She just sits in the water, soaked from the waist down.

Nell leans over her. "Are you all right, Anna?"

Anna takes the hand Nell offers and tries to stand

up. Whoops. Her feet slip again. This time both Anna and Nell end up in the water. They look at each other. Anna worries Nell might be cross. After all, it's Anna's fault Nell slipped, but Nell begins to laugh. Anna laughs, too. The two of them sit in the creek and laugh and laugh and laugh.

"Oh, dear," Nell says at last. "What will your aunt say when you come home soaking wet?"

Anna grins. "She won't say anything. She'll be laughing too hard." Though she doesn't say it out loud, Anna is glad Mother is in Baltimore. She would not laugh at the sight of a dripping wet daughter wearing overalls.

"Your aunt is a peach." Nell takes Anna's hand and leads her to the bank. Silver Heels lifts his head from the water and blows a puff of air through his nose. Nell nuzzles his head and gives him a hug.

"Such a good boy," she whispers in his ear. Then she boosts Anna onto the horse's back and leads him to the road. Nell climbs into the saddle and heads back the way they came.

Anna wishes the day would never end. "Will you come see me again?" she asks Nell.

"Of course," Nell replies. "We'll go riding again, too. Would you like that?"

"Oh, yes," says Anna. "Yes, I'd like that very much."

"Maybe we'll even cool off in the creek again," Nell says with a laugh.

Anna would like that, too. Her wet overalls feel nice against her skin.

Near the lane leading to Uncle George's farm, Nell points ahead. "Look, Anna. Here comes Mr. O'Reilly with the mail."

Way down the hill, Anna sees a big cloud of dust billowing toward them. She hears a loud chug-chug-chug. Out of the cloud comes the dirtiest, noisiest car she's ever seen.

Silver Heels neighs and turns his head this way and that. Nell clucks and nudges his sides with her knees. "It's just Mr. O'Reilly, silly," she tells the horse. "You see him almost every day."

When Silver Heels finally stands still, Nell slides out of the saddle and helps Anna down from his back. "Sorry," she says, "but Mr. O'Reilly's car spooks him. I'll have to ride home across the field."

Anna watches Nell leap into the saddle. Silver Heels

jumps the fence as if he has invisible wings. Nell turns and waves good-bye. Then she and the horse vanish into the woods like magic.

"Princess Nell," Anna thinks, "and her enchanted steed, Silver Heels."

Feeling a little lonesome, she trudges to the mailbox just in time to see Mr. O'Reilly trying to cram the catalog inside. "I'll take that," she says.

Mr. O'Reilly turns, surprised to see Anna standing there. "You must be Aggie's niece," he says. "Anna Sherwood, I believe."

Anna curtsies, showing off what she learned in Madame Tucker's dancing class. "And you are Mr. O'Reilly."

"Right you are!"

"The man who knows everything there is to know about everybody!"

Mr. O'Reilly raises his eyebrows, as white and bushy as Santa's. "Now, where did you ever hear such a thing?"

Anna giggles. "Theodore told me."

"Oh, he did, did he?" Mr. O'Reilly chuckles and fans himself with Aunt Aggie's *Journal.* "Well, well, I won't deny it. The only folks who might know more than me are the doctor, the minister, and the undertaker, but they don't talk as much as I do."

"Will you tell me some news?" she asks. "Aunt Aggie wants to hear everything you know."

"Well, now, let me see what's fit to pass on to a child such as yourself." Mr. O'Reilly thinks a moment. "Mrs. Baxter had her baby this morning," he says. "A fine healthy boy name of Daniel. He weighed almost ten pounds, and it took poor Mrs. Baxter twelve hours of hard work to bring him into this world. I sure hope the child's worth it."

Mr. O'Reilly pauses to swat a fly crawling on his nose. "Mr. Otis Crawford came home from his trip to Philadelphia with a bad cough," he tells Anna, "but Mrs. Crawford says he'll soon be on the mend if he just stops talking for a while. Mr. Joseph Benson fell off a ladder and broke his arm in two places."

Mr. O'Reilly swats at the fly again. "Pesky critter," he mutters.

"Anything else?" Anna asks.

"Oh, by golly, yes. The best news of all." Mr. O'Reilly tweaks one of Anna's braids. "Miss Eleanor

Bartlett has finally gotten herself a beau, a weedy young chap by the name of Henry Colston from Baltimore. Her folks are praying nothing goes wrong between now and the wedding. They need her bedroom so they can take in lodgers. They thought she'd never clear out!"

Mr. O'Reilly puts his car in gear. "Now, I must be off to pass on the news about you. But before I go, would you mind telling me the true story of how you got yourself soaking wet on a sunny day?"

Anna laughs. "Nell Webster and I fell in the creek together," she says proudly.

"You and Nell Webster, eh?" Mr. O'Reilly grins. "Now, there's a girl who won't wait long to be married. Why, I hear she's got half the young men in Prince Georges County courting her. The other half are either married already or haven't seen her yet."

Mr. O'Reilly eases the car forward. "Now, you tell your aunt everything I told you, Miss Anna. She'll be anxious to hear the details!"

Anna stands in the road and watches Mr. O'Reilly's car disappear over the hill in a thick cloud of dust. Anna can hear it long after it's out of sight.

She hopes she can remember everything he told her.

Aunt Aggie is so excited to see the catalog, she doesn't notice Anna's wet clothes. While her aunt thumbs through the pages looking for gas ranges, Anna tells her the news. Aunt Aggie is especially pleased to hear about the Baxters' baby.

"Mr. Baxter's been wanting a boy for a long time," she says. "Maybe now he'll quit pestering Mrs. Baxter. Six girls and one boy. Surely that's enough children for anybody."

Like Mr. O'Reilly, Aunt Aggie is happy to learn Eleanor Bartlett has finally acquired a beau. "Such a sweet girl," she says. "It's not her fault she's no beauty. We get what we get when we come into this world. And that's the truth."

"Nell Webster has oodles of beaus," Anna says.

"Indeed she does. More than you can shake a stick at." Aunt Aggie looks up from the catalog and stares at Anna. "Where did you see Nell? And how do you come to be so damp?"

"She came riding by while I was waiting for Mr. O'Reilly." Anna leans back in her chair and remembers exactly how Nell looked in her jodhpurs and jacket.

"She gave me a ride on her horse. Then we waded in the creek and slipped on the stones. We both got wet. It was so much fun we laughed and laughed."

Aunt Aggie laughs, too. "What a pair of silly geese," she says.

"Nell's the prettiest girl I've ever seen," Anna says. "I wish I could be just like her."

Aunt Aggie smiles and strokes Anna's braids. "You're fine just the way you are," she says.

"I'll never be as pretty as she is," Anna says sadly. "And I'll never have a horse like Silver Heels."

"Pshaw, Anna," says Aunt Aggie. "There's nothing wrong with your face. And we can't all have horses."

Anna sighs. No matter what Aunt Aggie thinks, she would gladly trade her plain freckled face for Nell's rosy face.

Just then, Theodore and Uncle George come stumping up the porch steps.

"Time for lemonade," Aunt Aggie says, running to fetch the pitcher.

Soon all four are gathered around the table, drinking lemonade and looking at the gas ranges in the catalog.

"Well, what do you think, George?" Aunt Aggie

peers at her husband, her small face tense with worry. "Can we afford a new stove?"

Uncle George leans back in his chair and lights his pipe. "The corn looks good this year. Prices are up, too. And the hay's doing well."

He pauses and Aunt Aggie leans toward him. She holds her breath.

"Yes," Uncle George says at last, "I think we can get the stove this fall."

Aunt Aggie claps her hands and runs around the table to give Uncle George a big kiss.

Anna cannot imagine being excited about something as boring as a stove. She hates to help Mother cook. When she grows up, she plans to eat all her meals in restaurants—no peeling or slicing for Anna, no stirring, no cleaning up, no dishes to wash or pots to scrub. But she's happy for her aunt.

And so is Theodore. "Hooray," he shouts. "No more wood to chop!"

◆ T E N ◆

Trouble in the Barn

ONE HOT AFTERNOON, ANNA AND THEODORE ARE sitting on the front porch, trying to stay cool in the shade of the wisteria vine. Anna is reading *Rebecca of Sunnybrook Farm,* but Theodore is bored. He says it over and over. "I am bored, I'm bored, I'm bored."

"Why don't you go inside and get a book to read?" Anna asks. She's bored of hearing Theodore say he's bored. Especially since she's perfectly happy herself. Or would be if Theodore would just keep quiet.

"Reading is something you do in school." Theodore scowls at Anna. "I hate school."

"Don't be silly," Anna says. "You can read anytime, not just in school." She shows Theodore her book. "This is a funny story about a girl who goes to live with her aunts on their farm. Want me to read it to you?"

Theodore stretches out on his back. "Go ahead," he says. "I ain't got anything better to do."

Anna loves to read out loud. Mrs. Levine told her last year she was very "expressive." Anna wasn't sure she meant it as a compliment, because she was frowning when she said it. In fact, Anna is almost sure Mrs. Levine meant she was showing off. But she decides to pretend it was a compliment, anyway.

Anna reads a funny scene to Theodore. Miss Dearborn is teaching Rebecca grammar, and Rebecca is having trouble understanding conjunctions, something Anna can understand very well. The scene makes her laugh so hard she has to stop reading till she recovers, but Theodore doesn't even smile. The expression on his face tells Anna he thinks the story is silly. Maybe he doesn't even know what conjunctions are.

"Do you want me to keep reading?" Anna asks crossly.

Instead of answering, Theodore jumps to his feet

and waves at two boys walking up the lane. "Homer!" he shouts. "Henry!"

Anna looks at the boys. Homer is tall and skinny and Henry is short and skinny. Otherwise, they could be twins. Their straight brown hair hangs in their eyes. Their ears stick out. Their teeth are too big for their mouths. They stare at Anna as if they've never seen a girl before. Compared with them, Theodore is a perfect gentleman.

"Who's she?" Henry asks, pointing a dirty finger at Anna.

"Her name's Anna," Theodore says. "She's from Baltimore."

"What's she doing here?" Homer asks.

Anna opens her mouth to tell him, but Theodore beats her to it. "She's visiting," he says gruffly. "She'll be going home Sunday."

"How come she's wearing boys' clothes?" Homer asks.

"Ain't she got a dress?" Henry asks.

Before Theodore can answer for her again, Anna says, "I have dozens and dozens of dresses. But on the farm I wear overalls. They're better for playing."

Homer and Henry stare at each other as if they've never heard a girl speak for herself. "Ma would never let our Lizzie May go around in boys' clothes," Homer says.

Henry nods in agreement. "It ain't proper."

Anna sticks out her tongue at Homer and Henry, but they have lost interest in her already.

"Let's go play in the barn, Theodore," says Homer. "We can swing on that rope your uncle tied to the rafter."

Anna knows perfectly well she should stay on the porch and read in peace, but playing in the barn sounds like fun. "Can I come, too?"

All three boys stare at her. Theodore looks embarrassed.

"We don't play with girls," Homer says loudly. He glances at Theodore and adds, "At least me and Henry don't."

"Especially not girls who wear overalls!" Henry puts in, speaking even louder than Homer.

"Especially not girls from Baltimore!" Homer hollers.

Anna looks at Theodore, hoping he'll take up for

her, but he just scowls. "Why don't you stick your nose back in that old dumb book?" he mutters.

Anna jumps to her feet, ready to tell him exactly how rude he is. But Aunt Aggie comes to the door and speaks to Theodore. "Anna is our guest," she says gently. "Let her play or come inside and sit for a spell."

Theodore draws in his breath to argue, but the look on Aunt Aggie's face tells him he'd be smart to keep his mouth shut.

"If I hear anything about your teasing Anna or being mean to her," Aunt Aggie adds, "I'll see that your uncle gives you a paddling."

"Yes'm," Theodore mumbles.

"That goes for you, too, Henry and Homer," Aunt Aggie adds. "I know your pa believes in the power of a good whipping."

Anna is pleased to see the grins disappear from Henry's and Homer's faces.

"Now, run along," Aunt Aggie says, "and have fun."

The four of them set out for the barn. When they are out of sight of the house, Homer turns to Theodore. "Has Anna played with your pet goat yet?"

Theodore grins. "Anna hasn't been near the barn-yard since she tangled with the rooster."

"You never told me you had a pet goat," Anna says to Theodore.

"I figured you'd be scared of him," Theodore says.

"Why would I be scared of a goat?" Anna asks. Ever since she read *Heidi,* she's wanted to be a goat herder like Peter and live in the Alps. She imagines herself leading her little flock across a peaceful meadow. She can practically hear the bells on their collars jingling. "I love goats," she adds.

"Come on, then," Theodore says. "Billy's pen is behind the barn."

"Billy is a boring name for a goat," Anna says. "If I had a pet goat, I'd call it Buttercup or Ivy or Morning Glory. Something pretty."

The boys nudge each other and giggle. Anna supposes they think her names for the goat are dumb. Let them think what they like. Why should she care?

As they walk around to the back of the barn, Anna smells a bad smell. She wrinkles her nose. "What's making that stink?"

The boys giggle again. Theodore points to a dilapidated pen. The ground is muddy inside. In one corner stands the most wretched goat Anna has ever seen. It doesn't look like the illustrations of "The Three Billy Goats Gruff" or "The Seven Kids" in Anna's favorite fairy-tale book. It doesn't look like Peter's goats in *Heidi,* either. This goat is skinny. Its hair is dirty, and its beard, so snowy white in Anna's pictures, is stained yellow, rather like an old man's tobacco-stained whiskers. Worst of all are its eyes. They're yellow and small and mean. It has sharp horns, too.

Anna holds her nose to block the scruffy old goat's smell. "That's not Billy, is it?" she asks Theodore.

Theodore looks offended. "Billy's no beauty," he says, "but he's a swell goat. You'll hurt his feelings talking like that."

"He's got the sweetest disposition of any goat in Beltsville," Homer adds.

"Why, he'll let you ride on his back just like a pony," Henry puts in.

Anna remembers how grand the world looked from the back of Nell's horse. But Billy isn't as handsome or as noble as Silver Heels, and she most definitely does not want to ride him. She doesn't even want to pet him. In fact, she wishes she'd stayed on the porch with her book.

Theodore grins. "Go on in there and let him sniff your hand," he says. "Pet him on the head. Once he gets to know you, he's just as nice as nice can be."

Henry is laughing too hard to say anything. Anna is sure the boys are up to something, but she doesn't want to look bad in front of Theodore. She goes a little closer to the goat's pen. Once Father took her to see the elephants at the circus. She wrinkles her nose. Even Billy doesn't smell as bad as they did.

"Just climb over the fence," Theodore says.

"Why can't I go through the gate?"

"It's busted," Homer says.

Anna climbs over the sagging fence, taking care not to scratch herself on the barbed wire. The goat watches her, but he doesn't move. He stays where he is, chewing something.

The closer Anna gets, the worse Billy looks and the worse he smells. More than ever she wishes she'd had the sense to stay on the porch.

"Go on," Theodore calls. "Or are you just an old scaredy-cat girl from Baltimore?"

Anna turns and glares at him. She's trying to think of a good insult, but her thoughts are interrupted by a loud bleat from Billy. She turns and sees him running toward her, his head lowered.

Nervously, Anna stretches out her hand to pet him. "Nice Billy," she croons, "nice Billy."

But Billy crashes into her and knocks her in the mud. Anna scrambles to her feet. The boys are howling with laughter. Billy retreats and then lowers his head to charge again. Anna runs. Billy runs after her. She screams. The boys laugh louder.

Round and round the pen Anna goes, with Billy close behind. Theodore has tricked her. Billy isn't his pet. He isn't nice, he isn't sweet, and he isn't tame. In fact, Billy's a lot like Theodore.

"Open the gate!" Anna yells at the boys as she runs past.

But they just stand there laughing.

Billy catches up with Anna and butts her again. Down she goes, flat on her face in the mud. Billy retreats the way he did before. He stares at Anna. Anna sits up and stares at him. As long as she doesn't move, the goat doesn't move. Keeping her eyes on

Billy, Anna scoots slowly backward toward the fence.

After a while, Billy loses interest. Turning away, he starts nibbling at a patch of weeds.

Anna reaches the fence and crawls under. Theodore, Homer, and Henry are still laughing. Anna doesn't even look at them. She walks toward the house, head high despite her muddy overalls and dirty face.

Theodore runs after her and grabs her arm. "Are you going to tell Aunt Aggie?"

"You lied to me," Anna shouts.

"It was just a joke," Theodore says. "Please don't tell. You heard what Aunt Aggie said. I'll get a terrible bad whipping from Uncle George."

"I hope you do!" Anna scowls at Theodore. "It will serve you right!"

"Oh, Anna," Theodore begs, "don't be mad. Billy didn't hurt you."

"Come to the barn and watch us swing on the rope," Homer says.

Anna hesitates. Part of her would truly love to see Theodore get another whipping. Before he tricked her, she'd thought they were becoming friends. Now what is she to believe?

But swinging on a rope sounds like great fun. If she tattles on him, Theodore will probably never play with her again.

Theodore tugs at her hand. "Don't you want to see the swing?"

Anna scowls, but she lets Theodore lead her toward the barn. She's been there before in other summers. The sun shines in long rays through the small windows high overhead. The shafts of light dance with dust. The warm air smells of hay and cows. Anna breathes it in, thinking how sweet it is, nothing like Billy's pen.

"See that?" Theodore points to a thick rope hanging from a rafter. The knotted end dangles above the barn's hard-packed dirt floor, much too high for Anna to reach.

"How do you swing on it?" Anna asks, truly puzzled.

"It's not for girls." Theodore begins climbing up a steep ladder that leads to the hayloft. Homer climbs up after him and Henry follows his brother.

Anna walks to the foot of the ladder and stares up. Although she would never admit it, she's always been afraid of high places. It's a long way to the hayloft, but if the boys can do it, so can she. She wipes her dirty hands on her overalls and grabs a rung of the ladder. Up she goes, hand over hand, foot over foot. Father once told her never to look down from a high place, so she keeps her eyes on the ladder rungs, but her back prickles as if gravity was pulling at her skin. Her legs feel shaky, too.

When Anna reaches the top of the ladder, she holds her breath and hoists herself to the floor of the hayloft. She lies still a second, hoping the boys won't see how scared she is. How will she ever be brave enough to climb back down?

As Anna gets to her feet, she sees Theodore reach for the rope. Homer grabs for it, too. "Let me go first," he yells. "I'm company!"

Anna shuts her eyes, sure both Theodore and Homer will fall to their deaths on the barn floor. Since Homer is at least an inch taller than Theodore, he gets the rope away from him.

"Watch me, Anna!" he yells. Gripping the rope, Homer walks to the back of the loft and then runs forward. Without slowing down, he leaps into the air and soars outward.

"'He flies through the air with the greatest of ease,'" Theodore sings, "'the daring young man on the flying trapeze.'"

Homer swings back and forth twice, but on the third swing he shouts a wild war whoop and drops into the hay piled on the other side of the barn. Anna watches Homer get to his feet and brush himself off. As far as she can see, he's still in one piece. No broken bones, no missing teeth, no cuts or bruises. He laughs up at Anna. "You want to go next?"

Anna glances at Theodore and is relieved to see him backing away from the edge of the loft, gripping the rope as if he means to keep it this time. He runs forward like Homer and flings himself into the air, singing the same song about the daring young man. Back and forth, back and forth he goes, and then, like Homer, he plunges down into the pile of hay.

"Four times," Theodore yells. "Beat that, Homer!"

Homer scrambles up the ladder with Theodore behind him. But it's Henry's turn now. He waves the rope in Anna's face. "You got to time it just right," he tells her. "If you swing back and forth too long, you'll miss the hay."

"What happens then?" Anna asks, feeling her knees go weak.

"You'll fall on the floor and bust your head and all your bones. Your innards will splatter like a tomato somebody threw against the wall."

With that, Henry goes to the back of the loft and runs forward. He sails out like the others, but after just two swings he lets go and lands in the straw.

"Cluck, cluck, cluck," cries Homer. "You big chicken!"

The rope swings back and Theodore hands it to Anna. "Your turn."

Homer snatches at the rope. "Give it here," he says. "Girls ain't got the nerve for stuff like this."

But Anna holds on to the rope. Isn't she the only girl in Baltimore who has skated down Bentalou Street, the steepest hill in the city? If she could do that, she can do this.

"Maybe you should give Homer the rope," Theodore says, suddenly worried.

Anna shakes her head and goes to the back of the loft. Holding the rope as tightly as she can, she wills herself to run forward and jump, just like the boys. But

at the very edge of the loft, she falters. Unfortunately, it's too late to stop herself. Anna sails out into the air.

"Let go," Theodore yells, "you're going too slow for another swing!"

But Anna's hands might as well be glued to the rope. While the boys yell, Anna swings back and forth in shorter and shorter arcs. Then she stops swinging and hangs at the end of the rope, looking straight down at the hard dirt floor. It's very far away. As Henry said, she's sure to break her head and all her bones, and her innards will splatter everywhere. She'll never see Father and Mother again, she'll never grow up, she'll never go to Paris. Tears fill Anna's eyes. Surely she's too young to die.

Just then Anna hears Uncle George shouting, "Hold on, Anna, hold tight!"

Anna turns her head and sees her uncle way down below. His two field hands are with him. They stare up at Anna as if they cannot imagine how a girl got in such a dilemma.

"My arms hurt," Anna cries. "My hands hurt, too. I can't hold on much longer."

Uncle George grabs a horse blanket and tells the

men to hold one end. He holds the other. The boys run to help. The blanket unfurls beneath Anna like a net.

"You can let go now," Uncle George tells Anna. "We'll catch you."

But it's not easy for Anna to let go. Surely the blanket is too small to catch her. She stays where she is.

"Please, Anna," Uncle George coaxes. "It won't hurt, I promise."

Dr. Thompson told Anna the very same thing when he gave her a smallpox vaccination. But it was a lie. Her arm hurt for days afterward.

Although she tries hard not to let go, Anna feels her hands slip a little bit.

"Jump, Anna," Theodore calls, "and you can have my share of cherry pie tonight."

Anna's hands again slip a little and then a little more. Before she knows what's happening, she's dropping through the air. In a second, she lands in the blanket and bounces once or twice. Uncle George is right. It doesn't hurt. No broken head. No broken bones. No splattered innards. Maybe Anna will see Paris, after all.

Now that Anna is safe, Uncle George hugs her tight. She hears one field hand say, "It's a good thing she's such a skinny little child. If she'd been any fatter, she'd have busted right through that old blanket."

By the time Uncle George lets Anna go, Theodore, Homer, and Henry are nowhere to be seen. They must have thought Uncle George would spank them all, Anna thinks.

The field hands go back to work, but Uncle George walks Anna to the house. Her legs are still a little shaky, so she's glad for the company.

"Did the boys make you swing on that rope?" Uncle George asks.

Anna shakes her head. "They said girls couldn't do things like that," she tells her uncle. "They said I didn't dare."

"So you just had to prove them wrong," Uncle George says.

Anna nods. "Don't tell Father and Mother about the rope swing," she says. "They'll never let me out of their sight again."

Uncle George laughs. "Your mother would have my scalp if she knew what you were up to."

Aunt Aggie is waiting on the porch. She's already poured three glasses of lemonade, one for herself, one for Anna, and one for Uncle George. "What was all that commotion in the barn?" she asks Uncle George. "I saw you and Elmer and Joe running like a house on fire."

Anna clasps her glass of lemonade and closes her eyes. She's afraid Uncle George will tell Aunt Aggie about the swing. Then Aunt Aggie will tell Father, and Anna will spend the rest of her life locked in her bedroom.

"Oh, the children were just making a rumpus in the hay," Uncle George says.

Anna opens her eyes just in time to see Uncle George wink at her. She grins and swallows a big gulp of lemonade.

"If Theodore was teasing Anna, I want you to give him a good thrashing, George," Aunt Aggie says.

"Theodore wasn't doing anything," Anna says quickly.

"Where has that boy gone off to?" Aunt Aggie asks.

"I reckon he went over to Homer and Henry's place," Uncle George tells her.

"I was so tired of those boys." Anna sighs and picks up her book. "Now I can read in peace."

◆ E L E V E N ◆

Market Day

*I*T'S THURSDAY NIGHT. ANNA'S WEEK AT THE FARM IS more than half over. Everyone is sitting on the porch, watching the stars come out. Anna is waiting for the moon to swing up above the maples. Soon she'll be sitting on the steps in Baltimore with Mother and Father, looking at the moon and thinking about her aunt and uncle and Theodore far away in Beltsville.

Just before bedtime, Uncle George asks Anna and Theodore if they would like to go to market with him on Saturday.

"You must go to bed very early tomorrow, long

before dark," he tells them. "And you must get up very early Saturday morning, long before sunrise."

Anna and Theodore look at each other and grin. Going to bed while it's still light and getting up while it's still dark is upside down, but it sounds like fun.

Friday afternoon, Anna and Theodore help Uncle George load his wagon with baskets of tomatoes, corn, potatoes, cabbage, peaches, and grapes. It's hard work. The baskets are heavy and the sun is hot.

After an early supper, Aunt Aggie sends Theodore and Anna upstairs to bed. It's hard to go to sleep. The summer sun slants across the wall and presses against Anna's closed eyelids. Birds sing. Uncle George's dog barks. The day's heat is trapped in the house. Anna tosses and turns. The more she tries to sleep, the more she stays awake. Finally, she gives up and begins to read *Rebecca of Sunnybrook Farm*.

Just about the time it gets too dark to read, Anna falls asleep. The next thing she knows, Aunt Aggie is shaking her shoulder. "Time to get up," she says softly.

Sleepily, Anna slides out of bed and gropes for her overalls. It's pitch-black darkest night. The moon is low in the sky, just above the apple trees in the orchard. There's not even a glimmer of daylight.

Anna and Theodore eat their breakfast. They are too sleepy to talk to each other, too sleepy to be excited, too sleepy to open their eyes all the way. Uncle George is outside, harnessing the horses.

"Run along now," Aunt Aggie tells Anna and Theodore. "Don't keep your uncle waiting."

Anna stumbles toward the door and staggers down the porch steps. Uncle George swings her up on the wagon seat and sits Theodore beside her. Taking the reins, he clucks to the horses. "Walk on, Bess," he says. "Walk on, Alf."

The horses are sleepy, too. They walk slowly, heads down.

"When will the sun come up?" Anna asks Uncle George. She's never seen a sunrise before, not once in her whole life.

"Sometime around six," Uncle George says. "By then, we ought to be in Washington, D.C., setting up my vegetable stall."

Anna rests her head against Uncle George's shoulder and watches the sky, hoping to see it turn pink. The wagon bumps and sways over the ruts in the road. Crickets chirp in the dark fields. A small breeze rustles the leaves. Slowly, Anna's eyes close.

When Anna wakes up, it's still dark. They are in Washington, D.C., just outside the market on New York Avenue. Uncle George's wagon is surrounded by other wagons. Horses stamp their feet and neigh. Chickens squawk, a rooster crows, geese honk. Farmers shout greetings to each other as they unload their fruits and vegetables.

"Wake up, you two," Uncle George says. "Help me set up my stall."

Anna and Theodore work so hard they miss the sunrise. Anna is disappointed, but Uncle George laughs.

"My goodness," he says, "don't fret, Anna. The sun will rise tomorrow and the day after and the day after that. Why, that old sun will go on rising long after you and I are gone. You can see it any day if you get up early enough."

All morning Anna and Theodore help Uncle George sell tomatoes and potatoes, corn and cabbage, peaches and grapes to city people who can't grow their own fruit and vegetables. Some of the women are cooks for rich people, and some are housewives like Mother. They squeeze the tomatoes, they peel back the husks and examine the corn kernels, they sniff the cabbage, they pinch the grapes. If they see a worm, they throw the vegetable back on the cart. If they find a rotten spot in a peach, they throw it back, too. They are just as picky as Mother, Anna thinks.

By noon, Uncle George's vegetables and fruit are sold. The customers are gone. At last, it's time to go home. Anna is almost too tired to eat the sandwich Aunt Aggie packed for her.

Before they leave the city, Uncle George drives the children past the Capitol and the Washington Monument. Neither Anna nor Theodore has ever been to Washington before. They have never seen such grand buildings. The white marble glows in the summer sunlight. Children run and play on the grass. Ladies and gentlemen stroll along wide paths. Pigeons strut at their feet, searching for crumbs.

As Uncle George turns the horses toward home, Anna and Theodore sit on the back of the wagon. They watch the Capitol shrink to the size of the tiny model

Aunt May keeps on her mantel as a souvenir of her one and only trip to Washington. Anna promises herself she'll come back when she's older and stroll on the shady walkways, taking in all the sights. Maybe she'll buy a souvenir and keep it on her mantel, just like Aunt May.

During the long ride home, the sun beats down on the fields. Theodore takes off his shoes and dangles his bare feet off the back of the wagon. Anna's toes feel pinched and her feet are hot. Like Thoedore, she takes off her shoes and lets the summer breeze cool her feet. How will she bear to wear shoes every day when she goes home to the city?

At last, Uncle George pulls the horses to a stop beside the house. Anna and Theodore jump down from the wagon. At the same moment, the kitchen door opens and out steps Father, shouting, "Surprise, Anna, surprise!"

Anna squeals with delight and dashes across the yard. Her bare feet fly over the pebbles and stones. She runs up the steps, way ahead of Theodore, and flings her arms around Father.

Behind Father, Mother cries, "Anna, what are you

wearing? What have you done to your hair? Where are your shoes?"

Anna steps back from Father and stares at Mother. "These are my farm clothes," she says. "Aunt Aggie gave them to me."

"I sent you here in a pretty dress looking like a lady," Mothers says, her face red. "And now look at you! Anna, what am I to think?"

Father starts to laugh. "We thought we were surprising Anna," he tells Mother, "but it seems she's surprised us."

"Indeed she has." Mother does not laugh. "Come inside with me this moment, Anna Sherwood."

As Anna follows Mother into the house, she hears Theodore say, "Is Anna getting a spanking?"

"No," says Father, no doubt disappointing Theodore. "I imagine she's about to have a bath."

"That's even worse than a spanking," Theodore says.

"Agnes," Mother says, "I cannot believe you permitted Anna to wear overalls and go barefoot. Why, she's not even clean."

Aunt Aggie shrugs. "Anna's in the country, not the city. Things are different here, Lizzie."

"But look at her face." Mother snatches Theodore's old hat off Anna's head and points at her sunburned nose and her freckles. "In Baltimore, proper girls don't get sunburned. They don't have freckles. And only servants wear their hair in braids."

While Mother and Aunt Aggie quarrel, Anna looks from one to the other. If Aunt May were here, Mother would have switched to German by now, but, like Father, Aunt Aggie doesn't speak any language except English. For once, Anna can understand every word Mother says.

Taking a deep breath, Aunt Aggie says, "A bath and a hairbrush is all Anna needs."

"The best soap in the world won't scrub off sunburn and freckles," says Mother.

"They'll fade," says Aunt Aggie. "In no time, Anna will be her usual ladylike self."

Behind Mother's back, Anna makes a face. She doesn't want to be her old ladylike self. She wants to spend the whole summer on the farm. Go barefoot every day. Wear raggedy overalls and braids and Theodore's old straw hat. Never wash her face or hands or take a bath.

While Mother brushes Anna's hair, Aunt Aggie heats water on the stove and fills a round tub in the kitchen for Anna's bath. She puts a screen around it so Anna will have privacy.

In Baltimore, Anna's house has hot and cold running water. She bathes in a big porcelain tub with claw feet. When she's clean, she pulls the plug and away the water goes, down the pipes with a loud gurgle and into the sewer.

"Scrub hard, Anna," Mother says.

Anna takes the soapy cloth from Mother and begins to wash. "Don't be cross with me," she says.

Mother sighs. "Oh, Anna, it's for your own good," she says. "I want to raise you properly."

Anna studies Mother's face. She wishes she could tell her everything she's done on the farm, but she's not sure Mother wants to hear about the goat or the rope swing in the barn or the day she went swimming in her underwear.

"I missed you and Father," she says, "and I'm happy you're here."

Mother kisses Anna's cheek. "I missed you, too," she says. "The house was so empty without you, so quiet."

Anna slumps down in the tub and stares at her knees rising out of the gray water like two skinny mountain peaks. "I must have been very dirty," she says.

Mother laughs. "You certainly were." She holds out a towel. "Now, get out and let me dry you."

Anna snuggles into the towel. She's glad Mother isn't cross anymore.

✦ T W E L V E ✦

The Church Supper

At five o'clock, Anna looks like a city girl again. She's wearing her best white summer dress, mended so neatly Mother hasn't noticed the torn places. Her hair hangs down her back, a little wavy from the braids but as smooth and shiny as Mother's brush could make it. A big white ribbon tied in a bow holds her hair back from her face, which is still freckled despite the lemon juice Mother scrubbed it with.

Worst of all, Anna is wearing shoes and stockings. Her poor feet feel cramped and pinched.

When he sees Anna, Theodore stares at her as if she's a stranger. A city slicker.

Anna doubles her fists, ready to punch Theodore if he says one mean thing, but he surprises her by saying, "Oh, Anna, I'd rather have a whipping than get all dressed up like that."

Anna pictures Theodore in a pretty white lacy dress like hers and starts to laugh. "I don't think anyone would make you wear a dress, Theodore!"

Theodore laughs, too. "You know what I mean."

Just then Aunt Aggie calls Theodore to come inside and get ready for the church supper.

Theodore tries to run away, but Aunt Aggie is too fast for him. She catches him by an overall strap and pulls him into the house. "You can't go to church looking like that," she says.

When Theodore comes back outside, he looks different, too. His hair has been combed, and his face and hands scrubbed. Instead of overalls, he's wearing a white shirt. His collar is starched so stiff he can barely turn his head. His white knee-length pants show off his skinny legs. His shiny shoes look as tight as Anna's. All in all, Theodore is even more miserable than Anna.

"It's only because of the food," he tells Anna. "Aunt Aggie said I won't get anything to eat if I don't dress up. Not even a piece of fried chicken."

Uncle George steps onto the porch. Like Father, he's wearing a suit, but his is black, not white. "Well, well," Uncle George says to Anna and Theodore, "look at you two, a perfect lady and a perfect gentleman."

Anna and Theodore both scowl at their uncle. They do not feel complimented. Neither wants to be a perfect lady or gentleman. What they want is fried chicken and potato salad, baked beans and pickles, corn on the cob and cole slaw, cake, pie, cookies, and homemade ice cream. If they must be ladies and gentlemen to get it, that's what they'll be. But only for tonight. Tomorrow they'll be themselves again. Or at least Theodore will. Poor Anna will be riding the train to Baltimore.

Uncle George drives everyone to church in the farm wagon. Anna and Theodore sit on the front seat beside him. Mother, Aunt Aggie, and Father sit in the back.

St. John's Church sits on a hill above the Baltimore Pike. Its red brick walls glow in the late-afternoon sunlight and its steeple pokes high into the sky. The grass and dirt around the church are full of farm wagons and automobiles, a Model T Ford here, a cart there. The horses wait patiently, their heads down. The women go inside, carrying covered baskets. The men stand around in groups talking. Boys and girls play tag in the graveyard.

Mother eyes the noisy children and takes Anna's hand. "Come with me," she says. "We'll help the women prepare the food."

Anna hangs back and watches Theodore run off to join his friends. She can't think of anything more boring than helping the women. "I want to play," she says.

"Those children have no manners." Mother holds Anna's hand tighter.

But Father comes to Anna's rescue. "Let Anna play, Lizzie," he says. "She can help the women when she's older."

With great reluctance, Mother lets go of Anna's hand. "Be careful," she says. "Don't tear your dress. And don't sit on the ground. You'll get a chill."

Anna promises to behave and runs into the graveyard to find Theodore. Homer sees her coming. "Look at you—you're a girl, after all!" he hoots.

Henry laughs and tries to pull Anna's hair, but she

ducks away. Both boys look almost civilized. Their hands and faces are clean and so are their clothes.

"Where's Theodore?" she ask Homer.

"Ain't seen him," he says and runs off with Henry in pursuit of a red-haired girl.

Anna searches among the tombstones. The farther she walks into the cemetery, the quieter it gets. Shadows stretch across the grass. The voices of the children are harder to hear.

Just as Anna's about to run back to the church, she finds Theodore standing all alone in front of a tombstone in a corner of the graveyard. On the grass in front of the stone is a handful of wildflowers.

Theodore glances at Anna and quickly turns his head. "What are you doing here?" he asks, keeping his face hidden.

Anna doesn't answer right away. She reads the names on the tombstone and picks more flowers growing in the tall grass near the grave. Quietly, she lays them beside Theodore's. Her heart aches for him.

"Is this your parents' grave?" she whispers.

Theodore nods and wipes his nose on his sleeve.

Anna draws in her breath. She cannot imagine anything more terrible than losing Father and Mother. Just thinking about being an orphan scares her. She crosses her fingers and says a little prayer, begging God not to let anything happen to her parents.

Slowly, Anna reaches out and touches Theodore's arm. He doesn't pull away. "You must miss them very much."

"I miss them every single day," Theodore admits. Wiping his nose once more, he turns away from the grave. "Let's play tag with the others," he says, running off. "The last one there is It!"

Because Theodore has a head start, he joins the game first, and Anna has to be It. But not for long. She's a good runner and soon tags Henry.

Theodore shouts and laughs. He makes more noise than anyone else. Whenever he's It, he chases Anna. But he never goes near the quiet corner where his parents are buried.

By the time the children are called inside for dinner, Anna has made several new friends. She has also lost her ribbon. Her hair is tangled. Her face is flushed. Her dress has a green grass stain on the skirt and the hem is coming out.

Mother is not pleased with Anna's appearance. "Oh, Anna," she sighs. "Just look at you. Will you ever learn to be a lady?" She tries to smooth the tangles from Anna's hair. "If you stayed here much longer, I'm afraid you'd turn into a regular heathen."

Although Anna has too much sense to say it, she'd rather be a heathen than a lady.

"Come get in line," Aunt Aggie says, taking Anna's hand. "And fill your plate."

The food is spread out on long tables. Anna has never seen so many delicious things. She piles her plate high with fried chicken and ham and corn on the cob, potato salad and fresh tomatoes, sweet pickle relish and baked beans and soft rolls.

Mother is horrified. "Oh, Anna," she exclaims. "So much food! You'll make yourself sick!"

Anna points at Theodore's plate, which is piled even higher than hers, and Father laughs. "They're growing children, Lizzie. Their stomachs can hold much more than ours."

Mother sighs. "Eat slowly, Anna, and stop when your tummy feels full. I guess it won't hurt you to gain a little weight."

Mother sets a good example by taking a small bite of Aunt Aggie's famous potato salad. "This is delicious," she says. "Would you give me the recipe, Aggie?"

"Of course." Aunt Aggie gives Mother a big smile.

Anna smiles, too. It seems her mother and her aunt are no longer cross with each other. Nor is Mother cross with her. Anna turns her attention to her plate and eats everything. When she's finished, she sits back and pats her stomach. She hasn't eaten this much since Christmas.

After dinner, Reverend Johnson finds two older boys to crank the phonograph. Soon couples begin to dance. Father gets to his feet and takes Mother's hand. He leads her out on the floor.

While a record of "The Blue Danube" plays, they waltz around the floor, gazing into each other's eyes but never missing a step. Father looks so handsome in his white suit. Mother looks so beautiful in her blue silk dress. Anna smiles. Her parents are the best dancers of all.

Aunt Aggie looks at Uncle George. "Dance with me," she says.

Uncle George's face turns redder than his sunburn. "Oh, now, Aggie," he mumbles. "You know I'm not one for fancy stepping."

Aunt Aggie jumps up and grabs his hand. "If Cyrus Skinner can get out there and dance with his wife, you can dance with me, George Armiger!"

Even though Uncle George is more than a foot taller than Aunt Aggie, he lets her have her way. Around the floor they go, rocking this way and that, bumping into other couples now and then, but dancing nonetheless.

Anna claps her hands and laughs at the sight of so many people having a good time. Fat men dance with skinny women, and skinny men dance with fat women. Short and tall, tall and short, they all spin past, laughing and talking as they go.

When she catches a glimpse of Nell in the arms of a handsome young man, Anna turns to Theodore. "Do you want to dance?"

"No, siree!" Theodore gets up so fast he almost knocks his chair over. Before Anna knows what he's doing, he's run outside.

She thinks about chasing him and dragging him

back, but it's dark now. Although she isn't scared of graveyards in the daylight, she's scared of them at night. If Theodore is hiding behind a tombstone, he can stay there. Let the ghosts get him. See if she cares.

Just then Father and Mother return to the table. Mother drops gracefully into a chair and fans herself. When Father picks up a glass of water, Anna remembers something she saw him do once.

"Father, can you still waltz with a glass of water balanced on your head?" she asks.

"I think so." Father glances at Mother. "Shall we give it a try, Lizzie?"

Mother shakes her head. "No, thank you, Ira. I'm much too warm to dance."

Father takes Anna's hand. "How about you? Will you be my partner?"

Anna curtsies, just as she learned in dancing lessons. "I'd be honored, Father."

When Father balances the glass of water on his head, Mother says, "Oh, no, Ira, please don't show off. You'll mortify me." But she laughs as she speaks.

Father just laughs and waltzes out onto the floor with Anna. Round and round they go. The glass of

water on Father's head sways a few times, but he never spills a drop.

When other people see what Father is doing, they stop dancing to watch. Anna sees Nell smile. She hears Mr. Skinner bet Mr. O'Reilly a dime that the glass will fall. She grins. Mr. Skinner is sure to lose that dime.

Round and round, round and round, Anna matches her steps to Father's. Mother may be red-faced with embarrassment, but Anna has never been so proud in her whole life.

When the scratchy old record finally comes to a stop, Father removes the glass of water and bows to Anna. He still hasn't spilled a drop. Anna curtsies again.

Everyone claps, except Mother, who is hiding her face behind her fan, and Mr. Skinner, who is reaching into his pocket for the dime he owes Mr. O'Reilly.

Best of all, Nell takes Anna aside to tell her what good dancers she and Father are. "And you look so pretty in that dress." Nell laughs. "The last time I saw you, you were soaking wet!"

"Shh!" Anna glances at Mother, but luckily she hasn't

heard Nell. She's happily gossiping with Mrs. Buell in German. Anna hopes nothing will be said about Cousin Herman.

To Nell, she says, "Is that boy one of your beaus?"

Nell giggles. "He thinks he is."

"He's very handsome," Anna says. "And he's looking at you right now."

"He is?" Nell blushes and leans down to whisper in Anna's ear. "Don't tell anyone, but I'm very fond of him. His name is Emory Harrison."

Anna grins. She loves secrets, especially romantic ones. "I think he's going to ask you to dance again."

While she and Nell whisper together, Emory Harrison walks up and asks Nell to dance, just as Anna knew he would. As Nell waltzes away, she blows a kiss to Anna, and Anna blows it back. Maybe she'll have a beau as handsome as Emory someday. Probably it will be Charlie Murphy. If he ever learns to dance, that is.

Anna sits down beside Mother. It's been a very long day and she's suddenly very tired.

Mother smooths Anna's hair and kisses the top of her head. "I think a certain little girl needs to go to bed," she says softly.

Anna nods her head sleepily. She's ready to go home now.

Taking Anna's hand, Mother leads the way to the wagon. Father and Uncle George follow. Aunt Aggie calls Theodore. He comes running from the graveyard, shouting good-bye to Homer.

On the way back to the farm, Anna sits on Father's lap. The wagon bounces, the horse's harness creaks. From the dark woods, an owl calls. Lightning bugs twinkle in the hedgerows like Christmas tree candles. Cicadas and crickets buzz and chirp. A soft warm breeze wafts the smells of honeysuckle and wild roses into Anna's face.

Anna shifts her position so she can see Father's face in the moonlight. He smiles at her. "Did you have a good time tonight?" he asks.

"It was the best night of my whole entire life," Anna says.

"Me, too," Theodore says. "I never ever ate so much good food."

"Just hope you don't have a bellyache tomorrow," Uncle George says.

"Even if I did, it would be worth it," Theodore says, stretching his mouth wide in a huge yawn.

Anna yawns, too, and closes her eyes. Her head bumps against Father's shoulder. She smells Mother's perfume, the lilac water Anna gave her for Christmas. It is truly the best night of Anna's whole entire life. She wishes it could last forever.

◆ THIRTEEN ◆

Home Again, Home Again

Sunday morning on the farm is different from other mornings. Although the chickens must be fed and the garden weeded, Uncle George does not get up before sunrise. He does not work in his fields. Instead, he sits down at the table and eats a big breakfast with everyone else.

"The good Lord got tired and rested on the Sabbath," Uncle George tells Anna. "What's good for Him is good for me. It's my day of rest, too."

"We have to go to church, though," Theodore whispers to Anna. "Which means wearing shoes two days in a row. I tell you, my toes will hurt for a week."

Anna sighs and smooths the skirt of her dress. She thinks sadly of the overalls she's left behind. "At least you'll be able to go barefoot tomorrow," she tells Theodore. "I'll be back in the city, wearing shoes and dresses every single boring day."

"Poor you." Theodore actually looks sympathetic.

"Come along," Aunt Aggie calls from the wagon. "Church starts in ten minutes."

Uncle George hoists Theodore onto the seat between him and Aunt Aggie. Father gives Anna a hand. She sits beside Mother. Their suitcases are already in the wagon so they can go straight to the railroad station from church. Anna turns around in her seat and watches the farm disappear over the hill. "Good-bye, farm," she whispers.

Mother strokes Anna's hand, but she's very quiet. Mother is worried, and Anna knows why. At home they go to Saint Gregory's, a Catholic church, but today they're going to St John's with Aunt Aggie and Uncle George. It's an Episcopal church. There is no Catholic church in Beltsville. Mother isn't sure Catholics should go to St John's, but Father says it's almost the same as St. Gregory's. He was an Episcopalian before he married Mother, so he should know.

No matter what Father says, Mother isn't convinced. But Anna thinks it's an adventure to go to a different church. She wants to see how they do things there.

Just as the horses pull the wagon into the churchyard, the steeple bell begins to ring. "Hurry," Aunt Aggie says. "We'll be late!"

Anna and Theodore jump down from the wagon and race each other up the steps. Uncle George catches Theodore's arm at the door. "Walk into church," he says quietly.

Anna is pleased that her family takes up a whole pew. Back home in the city she, Mother, and Father squeeze in at the end of someone else's pew.

The church is small and crowded and warm. People wave little straw fans to cool themselves. Anna sees many of the people she met at the dinner and dance. They are quiet and serious today.

Nell sits with her parents in the front row. Her shiny hair is piled on her head, making her look very grown up. Today she's wearing a pretty white dress with pink roses printed all over it.

Emory Harrison sits a few rows behind Nell. He watches her while the minister preaches. Anna decides he's definitely in love with Nell. She wonders if a boy will look at her like that someday. She hopes so.

Mother gives Anna a little poke with her finger. "Pay attention," she whispers. "Church is church."

Anna frowns and sits up straight. So far the biggest difference is that Reverend Johnson speaks in English instead of Latin. She tries to listen to every word he says, but the church is hot and stuffy and it's hard to pay attention. A fly buzzes around her head. She swats it away, and it lands on Theodore's nose. He swats it, too. The fly flits from person to person, causing a stir wherever it lands. Anna covers her mouth to hide a smile.

When church is over, groups of grownups gather outside to talk. The children scatter across the grass, laughing and calling to each other. Anna sees Nell with her family. She hurries to catch up with her so she can say good-bye.

"You're leaving today?" Nell asks.

"On the twelve-fifteen train," Anna says sadly. "But I hope to come back next year and stay longer. Maybe the whole summer."

Nell smiles. "I'll take you riding on Silver Heels again. And I promise you'll go home dry."

Anna hops from one foot to the other and claps her hands. "I love your horse," she cries. "When I get home I'm going to tell everyone about him and how we fell in the creek together. It was so much fun."

Out of the corner of her eye, Anna sees Emory Harrison lingering in the graveyard as if he's memorizing the names on the tombstones. "Emory's right over there," she tells Nell. "I think he's waiting to say hello to you. He was looking at you all during church. I doubt he heard a word Reverend Johnson said."

Nell blushes again. "Father says fifteen is too young to have a beau," she says. "If he catches Emory hanging around, he'll send him packing."

Anna pictures poor Emory leaving Beltsville carrying a little straw suitcase like hers, all sad and downhearted. "How old do you have to be to have a beau?" she asks.

"Eighteen," Nell says.

"Three whole years," Anna says. "That's a long time. You'll be a grown-up lady by then."

Nell sighs. "I know."

"Anna," Father calls, "it's time to go."

Anna seizes Nell's hand. "Will you write a letter to me?" she asks. "I promise I'll write back if you do."

Nell squeezes Anna's hand. "I'll get your address from your aunt," she promises, "and then I'll write you a nice long letter."

Anna hops up and down again. "Be sure and tell me all about Emory Harrison," she whispers. "No matter what your father says, I just know he's going to be your best beau."

Nell laughs. "You may be right."

Anna's father calls again. She gives Nell a good-bye hug and runs toward the wagon. For once she gets there ahead of Theodore. As she settles herself between Father and Mother, she sees Emory walking toward Nell, looking tall and handsome in his Sunday suit.

Anna nudges Theodore. "Emory's in love with Nell," she says. "And Nell's in love with him. But don't tell anyone. It's a secret."

Theodore makes a gagging sound to show what he

thinks of such foolishness, but Anna smiles happily.

At the depot, Anna and Theodore sit side by side on a baggage cart and stare down the tracks. Each hopes to be the first to spot the train, but they both see the smoke at the same time. They look at each other.

"Here it comes," Anna says sadly.

Theodore doesn't say anything. He jumps off the baggage cart and watches the train come closer and closer. Anna runs to join him, but he ignores her.

"Someday I'll go away on a train, too," he says. "I'll go much farther than Baltimore. All the way across the country, maybe."

Anna stares at Theodore. She wants to ask why he sounds so cross, but the train is making too much noise. The engine thunders to a stop, shaking the platform and sending up a cloud of steam. Passengers leave the cars.

It's time to leave. Anna hugs and kisses her aunt and uncle. "Thank you for inviting me to the farm," she cries. "Maybe I can come back next summer and stay even longer."

Everyone laughs except Mother, who blushes. "Anna," she whispers. "You mustn't invite yourself."

"It's all right, Lizzie," Uncle George says, grinning down at Anna. "We'll always be glad to have Anna visit. It was a pleasure to have her with us."

Anna looks at Theodore. He's still standing by himself, his hands jammed in his pockets, his head down. He isn't looking at Anna. This hurts her feelings.

"Aren't you going to say good-bye to me?" she asks.

"Good-bye," Theodore mutters. He still doesn't look at Anna.

The conductor calls "All aboard for Baltimore!"

Father takes Anna's suitcase. Mother takes Anna's hand. "Come along, Anna. We have to board the train," she says.

Theodore stands where he is, watching an ant crawl over his shoe as if that's more interesting than Anna. Anna allows Mother to lead her up the steps and into the train. She takes a seat by the window and sticks her head out to wave to Aunt Aggie and Uncle George. The train begins to move.

At last Theodore looks up. To her amazement, Anna realizes he's crying. He runs along beside the train, waving to her. "Good-bye, Anna," he shouts, "good-bye, good-bye!"

Anna begins to cry, too. "Good-bye, Theodore," she yells. "Good-bye!"

Mother pulls Anna back into the car. "You'll get cinders in your eyes doing that!" she scolds.

Father smiles. "I think Anna and Theodore will miss each other."

Mother pats Anna's knee. "Soon you'll be home with your old friends," she says. "Rosa will return from the ocean next week. Once you have her to play with, you'll forget Theodore."

Anna frowns at the thought of seeing snobby Rosa. All she'll do is brag about the ocean. No matter what Anna says about the farm, the beach will be better. Why can't Mother see what Rosa is really like?

"Charlie Murphy has asked about you every single day," Father tells Anna. "'When is Anna coming home? When is Anna coming home?' He sounded like a scratched record, saying the same thing over and over again."

Anna smiles. She'll be happy to see Charlie. But no matter what Mother thinks, she'll still miss Theodore. Maybe she'll write him a letter. Wouldn't that surprise him!

Before Anna knows it, the train is in Baltimore and she and Mother and Father are riding the trolley home. As they walk up Warwick Avenue, Anna sees Mr. Leidig rolling up the awning over the door of his bakery shop. Inside, his assistant is covering the display cases with sheets. The shop is closing. Too bad. There will be no eclairs or ladyfingers today.

"Guten tag," Mr. Leidig calls to Mother. "And good day to you, Anna," he adds. "How was your week at the farm?"

"It was wonderful," Anna cries. "I rode a horse, I swam in a pond, I danced with Father, I—"

Mother gives Anna's hand a gentle squeeze. "You mustn't talk the poor man's ear off," she whispers.

"But you didn't have a single chocolate eclair, did you?" Mr. Leidig asks.

When Anna shakes her head, Mr. Leidig runs into his shop and comes out with a white box tied shut with string. "Welcome home," he says and hands the box to Anna.

Anna is amazed. "Thank you, Mr. Leidig," she whispers. She wants to open the box and eat the eclair right away, but she knows Mother will say sweets are for dessert.

"I hope there's one for each of us," Father whispers to Mother.

"Anna's a good girl," Mother says. "And well mannered. She'll be glad to share the eclair."

Anna can tell by the weight of the box that Mr. Leidig has put at least three eclairs inside. She smiles. Sharing three eclairs will be easy.

She passes Beatrice's house and then Rosa's house. Neither girl is home. Too bad they can't see Anna parading up the street, holding her white box.

Just as Father unlocks the front door, Anna hears a shout. Charlie runs across the street, calling Anna's name. Quickly, Anna hands the precious box to Mother and races to meet him.

They stop in the middle of the street and stare at each other. Anna has forgotten how many freckles Charlie has. He seems taller than she remembered, too. And his hair is even redder than she thought.

"Guess what happened while you were away?" Charlie begins. "A house on Bentalou Street caught on fire. A streetcar hit the watermelon man's wagon and there were busted melons everywhere. Patrick broke his arm falling down the steps. A new family moved into the empty house on the corner. They have a girl named Dolly who knows swear words—"

Anna yells, "Hush!" She feels as if she's been gone for years and everything has changed forever. "Don't you want to know what I did on the farm?"

"Sure," Charlie says. "Did you see any snakes?"

"Not one."

Charlie looks disappointed. "Not even a little garter snake?"

Anna shakes her head. "But I got chased by a smelly goat and a mean rooster. I rode a horse and fell in a creek. I wore boys' overalls, and I went barefoot every single day."

Charlie's mouth falls open in surprise. "You wore overalls?"

Anna giggles. "That's not all I did," she boasts. "I went swimming in my underwear!"

Charlie whistles. "I wish I'd seen that! Woo, woo, Anna!" He grabs the ribbon in Anna's hair and runs off with it.

"Come back here, Charlie Murphy!" Anna chases Charlie. Nothing has changed, after all. Anna is Anna, and Charlie is Charlie, friends forever.